I0677439

K.O.'d
At
Banzai Pipeline

Also by Victoria Heckman

K.O.'d in Hawai'i Series:
K.O.'d in Honolulu
K.O.'d in the Volcano
K.O.'d in the Rift

Elizabeth Murphy Animal Communicator Series:
Burn Out
Wet Work

Stand Alone Mystery
Pearl Harbor Blues

K.O.'d
At

Banzai Pipeline

A K.O.'d in Hawai'i Mystery

Victoria Heckman

This is a work of fiction, a product of the author's imagination. Any resemblance to events or persons living or dead is entirely coincidental.

2016 Revenge Publishing
Copyright 2016 Victoria Heckman
All Rights Reserved
Published in the United States by Revenge Publishing
ISBN 978-0-9970880-0-7

Cover by Liam Heckman
Cover Photo by Mike Lopaka Jones, AZHIAZIAM
Author photo Blue Moon Photography

For all my students, past and present
who made their wishes known to be included in my
fictional worlds. You are all always with me,
as well as here in these characters.

6

Acknowledgements
Thank you to my very own K.O.—Det. Kathleen
Osmond of HPD, Ret. who always comes through
for me no matter how silly (or repetitive) the
question; Mike "Lopaka" Jones who answered a lot
of pro-surf related questions; and Jeanine West, of
the SLO Sheriff's Department Crime Lab who had
to change jurisdictions for this book! As always,
gratitude to my editors, Margaret Searles and Sue
McGinty, and foremost, my family. All of you are
critical pieces to this work.

I have taken liberties with the Triple Crown for plot
purposes, but the process of the final contest, the
Pipe Masters, is accurate as it is integrated into the
story. All alterations and differences are mine, not
due to any errors of the surfers I spoke to in creating
this work.

Nānā I Ke Kumu

Look to the source.

Chapter 1

K.O. stood on the slight rise above the crashing waves at Ehukai Beach, more famously known as the Banzai Pipeline on O'ahu's North Shore. Her fifteen year old nephew, Benjamin, nicknamed Raj, stood by her side. Both of them assessed the waves, but for different reasons. She, because she imagined the worst for her nephew in that crashing winter surf, as well as knowing she could never go in after him. And he, she knew from years of many similar experiences with him, evaluated each wave, each set, visualizing how he would approach and ride.

A few years ago, Raj had tied an old video camera in a Ziploc bag to the front of his board (after inserting a floatie-duckie) and filmed his day. The waves were nowhere near the height and fright level of these north shore December pounders, but viewing the footage had scared K.O. Besides, if anything happened to Raj on her watch, her sister Maureen would kill her. Even though K.O. was a Honolulu police officer, armed with gun, cuffs and other staples, she'd never be able to stand up to Maureen.

While the rest of the island went crazy with Christmas shopping, the surfing world went crazy readying for the last of the Triple Crown surf contests in a few days. Three of professional surfing's major contests were held here on O'ahu's north shore each November and December. Beginning with the Reef contest, then the World Cup, and finishing with the Pipeline Masters, this was one of the defining moments of a surfer's career.

Raj was one of the youngest participants (albeit an alternate), and had worked his way up over the years. He had entered lots of little contests and had been noticed by an up and coming local surf wear company, Bad Boyz Beach, who had really taken a shine to him. They had taken him under their wing and groomed him and now he was here. They sponsored a few other surfers, and Aliki Gomes was the oldest at 34. Aliki had made a lot of mistakes this season, so he had dropped down to an alternate.

"Look!" Raj pointed a tanned arm toward the water. "Awesome."

K.O. watched a surfer slide down the face of a wave and disappear into the pipe. A few seconds later he shot out, arms raised, victorious.

"Too bad was practice!" Raj slipped into Hawai'ian pidgin when he visited the islands. At home in Seattle, his mom would never let that happen. Maureen and K.O. definitely looked like sisters. Both fair skinned and freckled, but K.O.

had shoulder length red hair and Maureen's was short and blonde. Eyes were similar in shape and glare-factor, but K.O.'s were green and Maureen's hazel. Raj took after his dad Joe, a handsome Philippino with glorious dark hair and eyes. Raj's skin tanned, much to K.O.'s envy, because her own tended to burn.

"You going in?" K.O. asked.

"Yeah, I seen enough."

It was customary for surfers to watch the waves for a bit before they went in, evaluating sets and variations. Raj had already waxed his short board, so he tucked it under his arm and took off at a gallop toward the sea.

K.O. smiled as she remembered this same process over the years, the boards growing longer and then shorter as Raj got older and more skilled. Maureen's family visited often when the kids, Raj and his older sister Justine, were little, but as they got bigger with varied interests and increasing expenses, Maureen 'mailed' Raj out (the family joke) to visit Auntie. Justine surfed too, but as a hobby and less and less as she got older. For Raj it was an obsession; he was a true athlete and had dreams of winning the Pipeline Masters someday. Now that he was almost sixteen, he entered more contests, including the Hawai'ian surf contests— nothing this big, however. He had been to a few other contests in Australia and California, but mom wasn't really ready to let him go yet. The Triple Crown was the first set of contests that kept him away from home for a month. K.O. had promised he'd be home in Seattle by Christmas. She planned

13

to go with him and spend some family time—their parents lived outside Seattle on Mercer Island.

Raj had surfed in the first two contests, unremarkably, but was excited all the same. He'd retained his alternate status on the team, but none of his scores had propelled him into the running. This third one was his last opportunity of the year and required much more time and effort. K.O. had missed most of his previous runs due to the holidays creating the usual crime wave. She hadn't even met his sponsor yet, or anyone on the team. Raj's recounting of his days led her to believe he hadn't performed very well and didn't want to share. Now, however, he was revved up and she intended to participate more.

K.O. took a few days off whenever Raj came to visit, but since he was here so long, she spread her time off over the trip. She wanted to miss as few of his contest days as possible. From her condo in Kaneohe, he could jump on The Bus and get himself to the North Shore, no problem. No boards on The Bus, but his sponsor took care of him during practice. K.O. would make sure he had his own board when he needed it.

The sun beat down on the golden sand of Sunset Beach. More like light brown sugar than white, the long strip of beach glowed in the early morning, shadows long, as the sun rose. Lots of surfers and watchers milled around as the tents and structures of the sponsors and announcers were put up. K.O. moved into the shade of one of the palms at the crest of the beach and sat on her towel, binoculars in hand.

Raj hit the water and started to paddle, arms strong from practice. The waves were high but smooth and he easily split them or went over to get outside. The nice thing about Pipeline was the waves broke close to shore so the paddle out wasn't far, but that was also a danger. The long shelf that created Pipeline also meant surfers could crash in shallow water, easily breaking boards or themselves. The average was one fatality a year here. Grim odds. Raj shook his head to rid himself of those thoughts and let the joy of being in the water fill him.

Once outside the waves he sat up on his board and surveyed the beach. Lots of people already. He thought he could see his Auntie under the trees so he waved, in case. She always sat under trees or wore a hat because her *haole* skin burned so much. But she came out for him anyway. She hadn't watched much when he surfed the earlier contests—not that he was really *in* them—but now she said she was taking more time off work so she could be with him. He wanted to perform well for her.

He felt the next set building, rolling under him and he moved into position. The lines of surfers waiting for the set bobbed and weaved in the current. Usually he chatted with his surfer buds before the first set, but this time it came too soon.

The wave built from the north, rolling fast and hard. He looked back once and paddled, arms pumping, muscles readying to jump to his feet. The

15

swell pushed him and he was up. He towered above the watchers on the beach and rode the wave, through the pipe, a perfect cylinder for which the area was named. The wave closed over him and he was in the 'green room,' with only the rush of water and his ragged breathing that he felt more than heard, for company. He shot out of the pipe and turned over the back side of the wave and was free of the pull. His grin mirrored his exuberance and he glanced back at the beach. The little figure of Auntie was standing now; clapping over her head, mouth moving in what he knew was a raucous cheer. He laughed. He couldn't help it. The sheer joy of the ride, of surviving the ride, of the adrenalin coursing through him, bubbled up into laughter.

The sun beat down on him and he caught a few more rides, but none like that first. Raj checked his waterproof watch, one of the gifts from Bad Boyz Beach, and saw he'd been out several hours. He was hungry. And he felt a little bad that Auntie had sat on the beach and waited for him all that time. He rode a little foamy choppy roller into the beach and struggled up the sand to K.O.'s tree.

*   *   *   *

K.O. watched Raj approach shedding water like a puppy. She started to gather her things. "Great ride, little Dude." They often joked about surfing slang and other oddities of language. Raj might use it for real with his surfing buddies, but she felt silly calling his board a "stick." K.O. had surfed in the past also, but found the paddle out way too much work for what in her estimation was too little return for a short ride to the beach—if she was lucky enough to catch anything. However, she was an expert body surfer and Boogie Boarder. Still fun, less work.

"Yeah, was great!" Raj panted from his exertions. "I'm starved. You get anything?" Meaning, did K.O. bring any snacks.

"Not really. You like shrimp plate at the trucks?" K.O. referred to the shrimp farm on the way back to her house. Several food trucks parked on the pullouts near the farm and fresh fried shrimp could be had for a couple bucks.

"Oh, yeah. Onolicious!" Raj combined *ono,* the word for delicious, with the English word itself, like the ads did for the local restaurants. They walked back through the houses to the road. K.O. knew better than to park at Sunset Beach Elementary. The police were always alert and ready to tag and tow any surfing fans as soon as school administrators called. Although she was off-duty with Raj for a couple days, everybody else was still in school or at work. She felt like she was playing hooky.

They threw his board in the trunk of her Crown Vic. The lid didn't close so she gently Bungeed it shut. Raj had mastered the local manner of changing clothes in public by wrapping a towel around his waist, shimmying out of his surf jams, Bad Boyz Beach of course, and then putting on dry surf jams, also Bad Boyz Beach. Then he whipped off his towel like a magician.

17

"You like watch or what?" Raj joked, heavy on the pidgin accent. K.O. laughed. She enjoyed a unique relationship with her nephew. *Probably better than a parent,* she mused. She felt great love and great responsibility toward him, and they could talk about anything. She knew he told her things he didn't tell his parents. Ever since he was little and she first held him in her arms, she felt fiercely protective. She wondered if this might be what motherhood felt like, but she was in her 30s, and this might be the closest she came. Well, if things worked out with Alani . . . she smiled thinking of her handsome Hawai'ian boyfriend. Things had been rocky for a while, but now were smooth and . . . *don't go there,* she warned herself.

Shaking herself back to the moment she said, "Um, yeah, everyone like watch, brah. You standing on da side a da road." She used her best pidgin back at him. The traffic was bumper to bumper, although moving well along this, the only road that went around the north shore. It would become even more congested when the contest got going for real. Now it was mostly surfers, contest organizers and a few tourists ogling the huge waves. Soon it would be filled with fans and reporters as well as many more surfers, both contestants and supporters.

"Here, this will hold you." She handed him an Aloha Maid passion fruit juice, his favorite, when he sat in the passenger seat.

"Ah, Auntie, you da bes'!"

"I know." She navigated into traffic and they made their way to the shrimp farm and the wide spot in the road.

Chapter 2

After his shrimp lunch Raj wanted to go
back to Pipeline. "I wanna make sure everyt'ing's
ready, my papers and all."

"Okay, I want to do some Christmas
shopping, anyway. What time you want me to pick
you up?" K.O. knew Raj could stay all day. He
wanted to practice and he also enjoyed being around
everyone with the same goal—the contests.

"Um, five?" He raised his eyebrows. "They
said something about practice heats."

"Practice heats?"

"You know, for us guys who nevah
competed here before. We get forty minutes out
there and they do all the calling and we have to try
and catch something."

"Are you scheduled? Or are you just
showing up?"

"Scheduled." Raj squirmed.

"Why didn't you tell me this before? I can
be there, you know."

"I kinda nervous. Better you come later,
yeah?"

K.O. gave him her hard stare, the one she reserved for suspects. Raj squirmed some more. "Okay. But I'm supposed to watch out for you. If anything happens to you, we're both dead." It was an old joke, but they shared a smile.

K.O. pulled into the beach park parking lot. Several huge tents were up with sponsors' beach wear for sale, including a bright blue one for Bad Boyz Beach. A few food trucks had parked on the grass selling plate lunches, water and sodas.

"I'll see you later. Good luck and be careful."

"Laters!" Raj jumped out of the car and yanked his board out of the trunk, not even releasing the Bungee. He jogged through the huge welcome arch that listed all the previous winners and was quickly out of view. K.O. sighed and went around her car to remove the Bungee and slam the trunk lid. She had no intention of leaving him unsupervised. She knew he was experienced, an excellent swimmer and surfer, but he was only fifteen, well almost sixteen. He had his driver's permit and was already bugging K.O. to let him drive her car. That would never happen since it was department subsidized, but she had put in a call to Alani to see if she could borrow his second car, an old beater, a serviceable but scary-looking bright orange Toyota. They called it the Papaya since it was so bashed and bruised looking.

The parking lot was full so she pulled back out onto the highway to scout. About a quarter of a mile down she nosed into a hibiscus hedge and parked. Walking back a little she was able to cut through the hedge onto the bike and walking path that paralleled the houses between the road and the beach. Every few houses lay a public beach access path. When she came out at the beach, she was careful to stay in the crowd of watchers who stood like ducks in a row along the crest of sand.

It did appear that there were organized practice heats and it was only luck that she saw Raj struggling into a blue and white jersey. She never would have found him in the water if she hadn't seen him putting it on.

The breeze had picked up and the waves were getting rough. She heard over the loudspeaker, "Okay, guys, we're running this like the real thing. You won't be able to hear us once you're in the water, but listen for the horn. You'll get one when you start, and then half way at twenty minutes, and then when your heat is over. Come back in. Here's your line up." He listed several names including Raj, and added, "You'll hear your jersey color has priority and then you can go. You can lose priority by cutting off another surfer. We went over all this, but I want to be sure you hear me. Understand?" A little row of upturned faces nodded at the huge, multi-story media and announcer's box squatting on the sand.

"White jerseys, you're in, you have priority. Blue jerseys and blue-white, stand by for priority," came over the loudspeaker.

K.O. used her binocs to watch Raj. His face was tight with concentration, but he looked excited, too. The white jerseys went into the water and paddled out; blues and blue-whites stood on the beach with their boards, watching.

K.O. wrapped her towel around her. The wind had taken on a distinct chill and swept down the beach, west to east, same as the waves which had grown in the few minutes the announcements took.

The horn sounded and the white jerseys moved into position outside the line of waves. They bobbed up and down, straddling their boards, and a sudden quiet rose as the wind died and the sea grew momentarily calm between sets.

K.O. held her breath as she watched the ocean build behind the line of surfers. The crowd's excitement grew too, as they watched the first white jersey move to catch his wave. The wave built very quickly and he caught it, but misjudged the angle and as the wave continued up, the surfer couldn't cross the face and tumbled off his board. The crowd groaned but cheered when they saw him appear. A safety team in the water reassured K.O. as the white jersey paddled back out. While her attention had been on the first surfer, a second had caught a wave farther along and rode it out, cutting in and out and finally over the back side to tremendous applause. A horn call signaled change in priority and finally blue-white jerseys were in the water awaiting their waves. K.O. thought she saw Raj's board, but couldn't be sure so far away, even with her binocs. She vowed to get better ones by Raj's next day.

*   *   *   *

Raj's heart pounded as he tried to look calm on his paddle out. If he screwed this up, he was glad his Auntie wouldn't see it. He only recognized one other surfer, Aliki, also sponsored by Bad Boyz Beach. Aliki wouldn't even nod at him, so he didn't know what was up. Aliki wasn't super friendly anyway, but they were the only two guys from the same company on the waves. Maybe Aliki was nervous. He was much bigger than Raj, being almost twenty years older, well-muscled and tall. When Raj had first been recruited by BBB, Aliki had started off nice, but then gone cold. After that it was a guess as to how he would act the next time Raj would see him. Aliki was supposed to help him, according to Jet, the owner of BBB. Jet had said 'like a mentor.' Some mentor. Maybe Aliki was jealous of Raj. Raj wasn't as good a surfer, but maybe he would be someday, and Aliki was old for this competitive sport. This might be his last year. Getting a sponsor was tough under the best of circumstances.

The rising swell brought Raj back to the moment at hand. The set was building. During the two previous heats the sky had darkened and the waves had gotten bigger. The beach looked far away and the people were tiny. Even the huge announcer's stand looked like a toy from here. He faintly heard the horn and knew it was his turn. Now they were "in transition," which meant everyone was waiting for someone to catch a wave. He looked to his left. Aliki was two surfers away, watching him. Raj was on the western-most part of the line and would be the first to feel if the wave was right.

He glanced behind him. A monster swell was building. It was almost too close and too big, but he decided to try for it. He started to paddle and felt more than saw the others do the same. Because the wave was at an angle, many surfers could catch this one if they wanted. Clearly they did. If the wave wasn't right, they could drop out.

He felt the wave lift and he jumped to his feet. He dropped his weight back a bit and felt the nose of his board rise slightly. The wave continued to rise behind him, and the water above him felt greater than the water beneath. Not a good feeling; he thought he was too far down the wave too soon. The noise was incredible and he prayed he wouldn't fall with so much weight over his head. He turned his board a bit and was able to climb the face of the wave a little. It was bigger than he thought. He reached out a hand and stroked it down the wave as the curl enveloped him and he lost sight of the beach. He was far back in the tube and could see a little light forward of the foam. He worried it would close out before he escaped. For a moment he had the sensation of wanting to dive into the water, off his board and ending the suspense of *if* he fell.

Seconds later he was at the end of the tube and a figure rose out of the swell. Aliki. Aliki's board was sliding toward him, almost vertical down the face, and Raj was going to cross his path. Aliki saw him but it was so fast, neither had time to react much. Aliki instinctively ducked, and Raj swung his board up and above Aliki. The angle was too steep and Raj tumbled off his board and into the foam.

*   *   *   *

When Raj caught the giant wave K.O. stood and cheered, along with everyone on the beach. A few times she thought he would fall, when the water became so big behind him and he looked so far down the wave. He managed to climb back up, but was lost to sight in the tube. As she saw him exit the tube, another surfer dropped in from above, a safety and etiquette no-no. The crowd gasped as the collision seemed imminent. Raj somehow swung his board above the other and they missed, but Raj's angle was too steep and he fell. The wave had lost some of its power by now, but it looked pretty rough to K.O. The other surfer continued out of the wave and then cut back over the crest.

Raj's board popped up in the foam and his head followed a second later. K.O. breathed and the crowd cheered. The safety team had already moved toward him and helped him from the water. K.O. ran down the sand along with several contest organizers and a guy wearing a BBB tee and an embroidered tag that read, "Jet."

"Raj, you okay?" several voices asked at once. Raj looked a little pale but no blood anywhere.

"Yeah, I t'ink so."

K.O. grabbed him in a tight hug. "Did you hit?"

"Auntie? What are you . . .?" He gathered himself. "No, I missed him, but was close."

"What happened out there?" Jet asked.

"Dis guy dropped in and—"

"Who was it?" Jet asked.

Raj looked down and coughed a little water. "I don't know. Not sure, was fast, you know?"

K.O. was sure he was lying. But why?

"Okay, brah," said Jet, clapping him on the shoulder. "We take care a you."

"Who are you?" asked K.O.

"Who are you?" returned Jet.

"I'm Raj's aunt and guardian. I'm in charge of him while he's here." K.O. felt her hackles rise.

"Well, I'm in charge of him out *there,*" Jet said with a big, toothy smile. K.O. was not impressed. She glared. "Nah, nah, nah. I'm Jet, the owner of Bad Boyz Beach and his sponsor here at the contest."

Jet was about the same height as K.O.'s 5-7, but he outweighed her by fifty pounds or so. Looked like muscle, too. His dark skin had native tattoos on his arms and calves—altogether an imposing figure.

K.O. did not back down. "Okay, from now on, you let me know what's going on. And you make sure you do take care of him out *there.*"

"I'm fine, I'm fine." Clearly Raj did not like all the attention, and in this particularly negative manner. The horn sounded the end of the practice heat. He grabbed his board and slogged up the sand. K.O. followed him to the grandstand.

"I gotta find out how I did." Raj sighed. "Prolly not good. Maybe get kicked out."

"Why would you get kicked out? He dropped in on you." K.O. eyed him. "You know

27

who it was." It was a statement. "Why didn't you tell them?"

"I, I wasn't sure what happened."

"Sure you're sure. What gives?"

"It was Aliki. I don't want to cause trouble. He's been acting kinda weird and I'm not positive." He faced her, eyes pleading. "It's really big out there. You can't see anything. It probably was an accident. I mean, he could have been hurt too. Why risk that? I think . . . he just misjudged."

His face looked so downcast K.O. didn't press.

"Besides. What you doing here? You were going Christmas shopping?" The best defense is a good offense.

K.O. smiled. "You know how I feel about you," K.O. began.

Raj looked down, uncomfortable. "Yeah, yeah."

"If you think you were going to surf here all alone during the first official practice heat, without me here to watch your back, you mo' *lolo* den I am."

Raj smiled. "Yeah, you crazy all right."

"Besides, I'm not risking my best House Boy. What would Teresa say?" K.O. referred to her tabby cat who also adored Raj.

Raj was next at the scoring table. She wanted to eavesdrop but didn't. She backed off watching for signs of meltdown in his face.

He raced to her. "I scored highest in my heat! They didn't ding me for falling off after the drop-in because my ride was already over!" Raj was jubilant.

"Well, they shouldn't ding you for someone else dropping in anyway." She hugged him to her, not minding his sopping shorts. "What else do you have to do today? You done?"

"Yup, done for today. I'm starving."

"Let's stop at Foodland on the way home and get something for you to barbeque, okay?"

"Yeah, and something for dessert."

"Chocolate," they said together. They pushed through the ironwood trees back to the car.

"Reminds me of the pine trees back home," Raj said.

K.O. knew where his mind was going. "You can call home as soon as we get back, okay? Tell them all about it."

"Yeah. I will. And t'anks, Auntie."

"For what?"

"For being a big, fat liar and coming out for me instead of shopping."

"Anytime. I'm your biggest fan."

Chapter 3

After a huge dinner, Raj and K.O. lounged, sated, on her lanai. They watched the parade of little birds hunt for seeds and bugs in the grass below her second story deck.

"What's up tomorrow?" K.O. asked. "Only a few more days before the Pipeline Masters starts, yeah?"

"Yeah. More of the same."

"You okay? You don't sound as excited."

"I guess I'm a little nervous. Today was weird. Plus that was one huge wave."

K.O. sipped her iced tea. "Sure was. You think Aliki was trying to get in your way?"

"I been thinking. Not really. I think he didn't see me. On the back side it's really hard to see. The wave so big and so long, you can't always tell where you are on it, you know?"

"Mmm." K.O. tried to imagine rising over the crest of the wave to see a two or three story drop before hitting the trough. "What did your sponsor say?"

"About what?"

"Everything. Your ride, what happened, the contest . . ."

"He thought I did good. I didn't tell him it was Aliki. I no like make trouble for Aliki. He's having a rough time, so I wait and see."

"How does the 'alternate' thing work?"

"I ride all the waves and get scored. Then if someone is eliminated, my scores get into the mix. I score pretty good, you know." Raj rested his feet on the lanai railing.

"Yeah, I saw. How does scoring work?"

"You get points for the wave you pick, how tough it is, and the stuff you do on the wave."

"What kind of stuff?"

"You know, cutting in and out, over the crest, how long you in the barrel, when you leave the wave, stuff like that."

"How many points you get?" K.O. stood and grabbed the glasses. "Help clear up."

Raj also rose and moved to get the dinner plates. "Different for different contests. You get marked to 100th of a point."

"What's an average score?"

"I don't know. It's all different. I got a 4.83 for a qualifying ride one time."

"That seems low. Is it?"

"Not that day. I qualified."

"Okay, so a qualifying ride means you scored high enough to actually enter the contest?"

"Yes. Or if you're in the contest, then your score is high enough on the board to be competitive."

They loaded the dishwasher and K.O. wiped the table while Raj closed up the barbeque on the lanai.

"Sounds complicated."

"It's confusing. I'm new, so I'm learning all dis too. Just when I t'ink I get it, I wrong cuz some new rule comes up. Jet has to explain to me as we go. He tells me what's going on and what I have to do. He's really great."

K.O. saw his face light up when he spoke of Jet. She smiled at his enthusiasm, but couldn't deny a little wiggle of concern.

"What's next?" K.O. asked. "Movie?"

"Sounds good. But I want to call home first, okay?"

"Sure. Use the phone in my room. Quieter."

Raj came out sometime later and they settled to watch the movie of the week, *Point Break.* Kinda corny they agreed, but it was about surfing.

About the halfway point K.O. asked, "Popcorn?"

Raj nodded and K.O. went into the kitchen. The phone rang. "Get that would you, Raj?"

K.O. heard him say, "Oh, hey, Jet." Then the conversation became too mumbled to understand.

She brought the popcorn out in a big bowl to share. Raj was off the phone. "What's going on? Something with the contest?"

"Yeah. My score really moved me up he said. Also, the weather is going to get worse during the week, so he's gonna let me know every day if the contest is on or not."

"That bad?"

"Yeah, we're getting a week of storms he said. Dunno if it's gonna make the North Shore bad. Rain, no problem, but this is supposed to affect the surf."

"Okay. We'll keep an eye on it. I'm supposed to go in to work tomorrow. You okay with that?" Raj nodded. "I took a couple days off for the contest later in the week, though. I have a court date Friday, so I can't miss that."

"Court date? What'd you do, Auntie?" Raj teased.

"Ha, ha, very funny, doof. I have to testify against someone else. I spend half my life in court."

"I thought when you made sergeant you'd do less of that. Aren't you the boss or something?"

"Hardly. I got out of Records but part of passing the sergeant's exam is going where there's an opening. The opening was back in patrol, so here I am. Fascinating, yeah?"

"Oh, yeah. Poke me if I fall asleep."

"Anyway, I go in tomorrow and then I'm off 'til court Friday. I have a feeling this court case is going to slop over the weekend to next week. I hope not because you're supposed to surf next week, too, right? I can't take off days when I'm supposed to go to court."

"No worries, Auntie. I'll be fine. It all depends on the waves. That's why the contest dates are so long—to cover for bad waves and weather."

"Okay. I can drop you off at Sunset and then take the long way into work."

"No way. That's way too far for you. I can take the bus."

"If you take the bus, you have to borrow a board."

"Unless you want me to drop *you* off at work and give me the car for the day."

"Ha, you so funny." She ruffled his hair the way she had done when he was little.

*   *   *   *

K.O. dropped Raj and his board off at the beach parking lot the next morning with a few misgivings. She had known when she agreed to host him that she would not be available every day he surfed. More importantly, his parents were aware of that, too. However, she was not entirely comfortable leaving a fifteen year old alone all day at the beach. Okay, not alone-alone. Hundreds of people would be there, but none of them had only his interests at heart. Jet, and BBB, were somewhat invested, she admitted grudgingly, as she entered the little town of Haleiwa on her way to the H-2 freeway. He would be fine. She had admonished him to call her from the park pay phone if anything came up, and she had already planned to leave a little early to beat the terrible commuter traffic leaving Honolulu for points west in the afternoon. She could make the north shore in an hour if traffic cooperated. Today was a paperwork day so if all went well . . .

*   *   *   *

A light, warm breeze shifted the palm fronds and ironwood needles as Raj made his way to the check-in area. He looked for Jet but didn't see him. Another day was gearing up and he felt the excitement building around him. The light brown-sugar sand was cold under his feet. The sun was up but not high enough to warm the beach past the jagged green ridge of mountains. He got a brief whiff of morning bacon from somewhere in the row of houses next to the beach. Already people sat in their yards or on their lanais with coffee, prepared to watch another day of surfing. Again he was assigned a blue-white, slightly damp jersey and shivered as he put it on. Usually a different jersey color was assigned, so maybe this was a good sign.

"Okay, you're up in the third heat," said the guy with the list. Ragged blond hair and a Billabong tee accompanied his mandatory surf jams.

"My practice heat, you mean?" Raj asked.

"No, brah, your qualifying heat."

"What do you mean, 'qualifying heat'?" Raj's mouth went dry.

"You gotta qualify." Raj didn't respond. "You know, see if you *in,* brah."

"I'm only an alternate," Raj practically squeaked. His voice had changed when he was thirteen, but now it sounded weird again.

"Yeah, I know. You still gotta qualify. What if someone drops out? All your scores come into da mix. How come no one told you nothing?"

"What do I do now?"

"If I was you, brah, I find my sponsor real

quick and find out what da hell's going on. Den I get ready to qualify. Good luck. Next!"

Raj staggered away from the check-in area and plopped on the beach. The same jersey color didn't quite cut it for good omens. The long shadows of early morning that had left the whole beach in shade began to recede. The water sparkled more green than blue and the waves rolled in smooth and glossy today. That would probably change as the day progressed. The sky was clear to the north, no sign of a storm.

"Hey, you okay?" A teenaged girl dropped onto the sand next to him.

"I guess so." Raj looked at her. She wore BBB surf wear, too.

"What's wrong?"

"Who are you?" Raj asked.

"Oh, sorry. I'm Kahana. I surf for BBB, too. I've seen you around. You the new Golden Boy from what I hear."

"Um, okay." Raj was uncomfortable. He noticed Kahana's long dark hair with bangs that stopped above straight dark brows. Her eyes were light brown with flecks of green. Pretty. "How long you been with BBB?"

"Coupla years, I guess. I been doing pretty good. I placed in the women's competition last week and came out to support the team." She studied him. "What's up with you? Sick or something?"

"No. I just thought today was a practice heat, like yesterday, but it's a qualifying round."

"So?"

"So. I don't know. I guess I don't feel ready. Nobody told me. Woulda been nice."

"When you gonna feel ready?" She smiled to take the sting out.

"Never?" Raj smiled back.

"Right. You never feel ready the first time." She flicked sand on him with her foot. "It's your first time, yeah?"

"Yeah. For a contest this big. Triple Crown. Whoa."

"My first advice is not to think about how big this contest is. Next, get your head in the waves. See, look." She stood and led him closer to the water, at the crest of the beach.

"Watch the sets. Right now, is good. Sets smooth and big. Maybe not as many points, but a good way to start. What heat?"

"Third."

"That's good, too. Should still be smooth this morning. When you get into the afternoon, sometimes everything changes. You know, weather and wind."

"Supposed to get one storm, but looks clear," Raj said.

"Try look." Kahana turned to look south over the mountains. The whole sky was gray. "We be lucky to finish today. I bet you tomorrow is cancelled. I heard small craft advisory on the radio."

A horn sounded and they heard, "White jerseys, in the water. Whites you have priority. Yellows and blue-whites stand by."

"Here we go," said Raj.

"Here *you* go," said Kahana. "I'll watch you, okay?"

"Okay." Their eyes met.

"Trust yourself. You can do it."

Raj inhaled deeply and nodded. He almost wished his Auntie was here. Or his dad. His dad was his first teacher and biggest supporter. He moved off down the beach toward a small cluster of blue-white jerseys, board tucked under his arm.

He didn't remember the white jerseys surfing at all. He knelt and waxed his board, a little island in the sea of colored jerseys and excitement. He came around when the yellows were called to the water and his color, blue-white, was on stand-by. He shook himself a little and concentrated on the water. The waves looked good. Not too choppy. He knew he'd get creamed if he didn't pay attention. The ocean was unforgiving of mistakes and some could be fatal. He always had one moment when he was surfing, of feeling in total control, and another moment of complete lack of control. That balance kept him going, but it also scared him.

Once a guy right next to him on a wave fell and broke his arm and his board. Raj had surfed on by without realizing the guy was hurt. It had been a nothing day. Nothing special, nothing unusual, but things change in an instant out there.

His mind had wandered again. Frustrated he faced the water and watched the sets. Too distracted. That's how accidents happen.

A smattering of applause signaled a good ride for a yellow jersey. The horn. During the previous two forty-minute heats the wind had picked up. The down time between heats didn't help when the weather was shifty. Blue-whites were called to the water and Raj tucked his board and headed out. The waves were bigger, too. Not his imagination. He felt the tension in the little blue-white group. Something in the set of their shoulders as they walked and then paddled. The water felt really cold as he waded out and lay on his board. Even between sets, the swell made paddling tougher. The inviting green water of the early morning had given way to a blue-gray that matched the darkening sky.

Relax. Focus. Paddle. His arms moved in rhythm, strong pulls moving him beyond the wave line. A set began and he sat up on his board to watch. He was not in a good position and adjusted. He also was not on the end this time. The line was strung pretty far apart. At some contest locations, the waves were short and the surfers sat practically on top of each other. Surfers were territorial and fights often broke out both in the water and on the beach about perceived slights and possession of waves. Pipeline was nice and long and if the judges could see you, it was all good.

The horn signaled the beginning of the heat. All the surfers had the same amount of time to catch a wave. Choosing the right wave was halfway to winning, Jet always said.

A few surfers caught waves from this first set. Okay rides in Raj's opinion, but not great. Apparently the surfers thought so too as they cut over the back side to line up again. A lull between sets. Raj felt his stomach flip. He'd have to take a wave in this set. He was running out of time. The sets were about 20 minutes and he'd sat out the first set.

The second set built behind him but he quickly saw it was rougher and darker than the set even a few minutes ago. A wave towered above him but was already curled and toppling and carried several surfers on it. He ducked under and felt the power of it as it passed over, trying to take him with it. He pushed down farther and felt something bump his board as he struggled to stay submerged. *Hope I didn't ruin someone's only ride.* That thought flashed through him even as he realized it would be a competitor.

He popped up, the wave continued on its way, the mass of it blocking Raj from seeing who he might have affected. He looked back to check the set. A wave built before his eyes and he had no time to think. He faced the beach and paddled as a giant roller tried to pick him up. He almost gave up on it, but knew if the judges thought he had committed and then backed out, they would take points he couldn't afford. He stuck to it. It felt a hundred feet high. Because it was not one of the whole-beach-long waves, Raj felt like all that energy was compressed into a short, chubby killer wave, like the cartoon waves with minds of their own that attacked people.

It swept him up to its crest and Raj fought to stay up. It didn't behave like the waves he was used to. Must be the storm. Chunks of water, no other way to describe them, popped up like speed bumps, and he cut up and down, in and out like a skier around moguls. He felt the wave get narrower, if that was possible, raising more water and pulling him even higher. His peripheral vision saw nothing but a blue wall. No green room even, no tube. Just a big wall without sky and beach. He was sliding down a waterfall and all he could do was hang on.

He didn't remember much after the blue wall. He didn't fall, he knew that. He was hanging on so tightly with feet, and weight, balance and sheer will, that he didn't leave the wave, but rode it all the way in.

It was fortunate that he had, because the weather and water conditions degraded so radically during his ride that the rest of the day was cancelled. When he hit the beach and looked back, the water was black and swirled with chop. Surfers tried to ride back, but many gave up and paddled. A few other surfers had also caught his wave, but had dropped out or fallen. No injuries luckily.

Kahana ran to meet him. "That was awesome! I can't believe you rode that." Her eyes were bright and her hair flew around her head like a halo.

"Was weird, all right." Raj shivered in the icy breeze.

Kahana handed him a towel. "Let's go see the scores. Oh, my god, it's cold. You must be freezing!"

"Yeah." Raj stuck his board in the sand and rubbed briskly with the towel to warm up. He handed her back the towel and picked up his board. "What time is it? I'm starved."

"Almost noon. Not that late. Weather's crap, though. Look at those waves."

They stopped and looked. Very strange. Almost flat black water, and then a choppy foamy wave would rise and crash its way to the beach. A few of those and then nothing.

"Sheesh. I'm glad I got my ride in."

"Me, too. Lessee what they say."

They made their way to the judges' stand. As they got to the front of the line, the loudspeaker announced the scores. "Buddy Soarez 3.83, Tai Phillips 3.84, Aliki Gomes 5.22 and Raj Dela Cruz 6.76."

"Holy cow! You got the high score for your heat!" Kahana jiggled in excitement.

"Yeah, but you know, not everyone got a ride. Maybe they get higher scores tomorrow." Raj tried to sound humble but was jubilant. "Gotta call my Auntie."

"Okay. Then let's get a plate lunch. My treat."

"Sounds good, thanks." They walked to the park where the food trucks parked and ordered. While they waited for their food, Raj called K.O.

Chapter 4

K.O. sat in court, blue wool uniform itchy and uncomfortable. At least the courtroom was air conditioned so she wasn't overheated, as often happened to her out in the city. *I don't know why we don't all get heat stroke or change the stupid uniform policy*, she moaned to herself fruitlessly for the thousandth time since she began her career with HPD.

Her case was a traffic stop, straightforward and fast. Soon she was back at her desk mired in paperwork. Her stomach rumbled as lunch time approached and her phone rang.

"Sergeant Ogden," she answered.

"Hey, Auntie! Guess what? I qualified!" Raj's excitement spilled out and K.O. laughed.

"I didn't even get to guess," she said.

"Fo' shua," Raj said. "The rest of the day's cancelled. When you *pau*?"

K.O. glanced at the clock. "I'm done now, pretty much. I had my court case and am catching up on paperwork. I could be enticed into stopping that, however."

43

"I'm starving. You can get me, or what?"

"Sure. It'll be a while. Why don't you catch The Bus toward Kaneohe and I'll drive up from here and pick you up at the usual stop?"

"Sure." Raj and K.O. had worked out this system many visits ago. The Bus that went around the island (helpfully called Circle Island) had one road and one route around the North Shore. Even when Raj was younger, K.O. had felt safe putting him on it and asking the drivers to watch out for him.

"Why cancelled?" K.O. asked. "Something happen?" In K.O.'s mind something had always happened. Well, it was her business, too.

"You get windows down there, Auntie, or are you in jail again?"

"Very funny. No, in my office." She glanced out her south-facing windows. Dark sky. Clouds were indistinguishable, only a wall of gray. "Wow. I guess that storm pushed up. Okay, I'm on my way. Where you now?"

"Still at Sunset. I gonna grab a plate lunch and den hop Da Bus."

"You're going to have a plate lunch before we have lunch? Nevermind." K.O. heard his laughter. He knew how she would respond. She wasn't scolding; she knew he used a lot of energy out there, and growing boys ate all the time anyway. Their relationship was founded on love, but lived on humor. "Stay dry. See you in a bit."

They disconnected and she grabbed her purse. She had forgotten a jacket, but that was fine since she could access the police garage from inside the building. She kept a windbreaker and umbrella in her car.

The weather had devolved by the time she drove out of the parking garage and headed toward the brand spanking new H-3 freeway. It had literally just opened and she had only been on it twice. Still a novelty for the islanders, it had plenty of its own traffic, but that would settle. Before H-3, she had to take the Likelike highway and although scenic, it was narrow and rush hour was no fun. H-3 should alleviate a lot of that traffic. Likelike dumped her out closer to her townhouse, but now she was going north to meet The Bus and Raj, so H-3 was the logical choice. She didn't really need an excuse to take the new road. It was a miracle of engineering and was so . . . new. The view out of the tunnels to the Windward side and Kaneohe Marine Corps Air Station was spectacular. The wide lanes wound down the green mountains to the sea. Breathtaking.

The sky was nearly black and rain began to spatter her windshield in earnest. Although it was the middle of the work day, a lot of folks had the same idea to get out of Dodge. It was slow going on H-1 until she passed the exit for Likelike toward Pearl City and H-3. Then she was able to go freeway speed all the way through the tunnels. She slowed as the road sloped steeply downhill, but she had beaten the rain to the windward side. She hoped Raj had stayed dry while he waited for The Bus. Rain was frequent here, so many of the bus stops had shelters. Didn't help much when the rain blew sideways as it began to now. Rats.

She hit the narrow, winding coastal road, usually so beautiful right next to the ocean, but now waves splashed to the northbound, *her,* lane. She stayed as far from the water as possible, but southbound traffic was heavy as people left the North Shore. She had not seen the familiar shape of the yellow, black and white Bus yet and was getting concerned. Visibility had decreased making driving stressful. Her palms wet the steering wheel. Headlights did nothing. The thought of the bus driving into the ocean, only feet away, kept her going. She didn't want Raj on that bus one minute longer than necessary.

She made it to Laie and pulled off into the bus stop at the Polynesian Cultural Center. It was farther back from the ocean and she felt safer. This was their usual meeting spot. He could walk to the A & W restaurant and get food while he waited for her. Now, however, it looked like everything was shut down with the approaching storm. It was worse than she thought. She hadn't seen a bus yet. Could he have caught one right away and be ahead of her? It was so dark and rainy, maybe she missed it? What if the weather was so bad, they cancelled the buses? She hadn't even looked at the schedule before she left. Maybe in the glove box. Or had she given it to Raj? She pawed open the glove compartment just as headlights flashed. The Bus!

She flashed her own lights in case Raj couldn't see her in the storm, but dimly she saw a figure shoot out the accordion doors and straight toward her car.

"Whoa, dat was something!" Raj's sopping body spattered her as he threw himself in the seat.

"I was getting a little worried." Major understatement. "Everything all right?"

"So exciting! Yeah."

"Um, where's your board?"

"I gave to Jet. He's gonna put it in the house for me."

"What house?"

"Oh, the BBB house. They rent a house for all the guys who don't have a place to stay and there's like, a chaperone there. Anyway, he said I could stash it there."

This was the first K.O.'d heard of a 'team' house. "Okay. Wow, this is terrible. I was really worried about you for a bit."

"Hoooeee!" Raj let out, startling K.O.

She looked at him in disbelief, then screamed, "Whooo hoooo!"

The burst of adrenaline combined with the tense drive let go all at once. They sat in the car laughing like lunatics. She turned on the heater and then the defroster as Raj's wet jams and their whoops fogged up the windshield.

"Okay, brah, you ready for dis?" K.O. asked as she put the Crown Vic into drive.

"You bet. Less do um."

"At least we're on the inside lane now. If the road's still there." K.O. thought furiously. What was her plan B if the road was really awash, or literally washed away? The homes along the highway wouldn't be any refuge at all. She had nowhere to go.

She pulled into the road and headed south. A tug of concern when she saw no other traffic. No Bus, so maybe headed back north. She was lucky to get Raj when she did. All the cars she'd seen on her way up had evaporated. Or washed into the sea. Even Raj was quiet as she negotiated the tight turns and sheets of rain. She hugged the outside white line of the lane and drove constantly through several inches of water. No huge waves crashed over the car, but would she see them coming anyway? The long drive took even longer at no miles an hour. She was afraid of losing traction and afraid she wouldn't see if the road had washed out and she was about to drive into the water. They passed Punaluu Beach Park, the sign barely registering. Then Kaaawa. Beyond that, the road curved a bit away from the ocean. K.O. pulled over and exhaled.

"What's wrong?" Raj asked.

"I need a minute." K.O. shook her hands which had started to cramp up on the wheel. She rubbed them on her pants. The sound of the rain was incessant and deafening. The Crown Vic's large engine was no match for the storm. Raj watched her, eyes big.

"It's going to be fine. We're almost there. We're past the worst of it." That wasn't exactly true, but Raj looked relieved.

Carefully she pulled back onto Kam highway and ironically, the storm subsided a little. She wished it hadn't because of what she saw. The waves now rolled over the highway, deeper than they had before. If she didn't know this road so well, it would be easy to end up swimming. She

48

should have stayed where they were. No way she could turn around on the narrow road and go back. Earth and sky, water and waves all blended together. She used the vegetation on her side of the road as a guide. She drove at a crawl until Waiahole where the road turned away from the ocean again.

Now she really knew where they were. Almost home. Right now, the terrain didn't look at all familiar, but she drove this part almost every day. Not a time to speed up, but her frame of mind improved. One more sketchy spot and the highway split into two: Kam highway along the ocean and Kahekili highway inland toward her townhouse.

She glanced at Raj and saw he also knew where they were. She realized she really had to go to the bathroom at the same time Raj said, "I gotta pee, I so nervous."

That broke the tension and they discussed that topic until they reached her place. Fortunately she had two bathrooms so a fist fight did not ensue.

When they were relieved, dry and rummaging for food, she said, "We will never speak of this."

Raj nodded solemnly, knowing that declaration referred solely to his mother. "No way, brah. We didn't die in the storm jus' so she could kill us later."

Chapter 5

      K.O. and Raj had fallen into an exhausted sleep after their circle island tour during the storm. After they had made it home and eaten, they passed out. K.O. awoke later to find the electricity out, so she retrieved candles and flashlights and place them around the townhouse. Raj didn't awaken as far as she could tell. Still tired, she fell back to sleep. The electricity came back during the night so the morning brought daylight with all her lights on.

      "Yeah for Hawaiian Electric," K.O. praised the company for getting them back online.

      "Fo' sho," Raj agreed. He appeared in the guest room doorway, scratching his dark hair 'til it stood up in brushy clumps. He looked about four years old and reminded K.O. of a photo she had of him early one morning at that age, wearing black PJs with "BOO!" across the tummy.

      "So cute," she muttered.

      "What?"

      "Nothing. You hungry?"

      "Of course." Raj continued to the bathroom.

"Of course," K.O. echoed. Teresa, her tabby kitty deigned to make an appearance after sleeping next to K.O. on a pillow. The storm had been noisy, and even though Teresa usually slept on K.O.'s bed, she had been positively cuddly last night.

"Well, hello your majesty. You hungry, too?" Teresa's waving tail wrapped neatly around her and she sat expectantly next to her bowl. K.O. got her fresh kibble and water and a spoonful of wet food that always smelled disgusting to K.O., but Teresa had nothing but praise for it. K.O. had rescued Teresa and her litter of newborns from the shrubs outside her condo several years ago. She hadn't been looking for a pet, but Teresa had other plans and they made a companionable team. Teresa didn't mind too much when K.O. had to work late, or for days in a row. K.O.'s neighbor had an emergency key and Teresa came and went from the pet door installed in the slider on the second floor lanai. K.O. had worried at first that Teresa would get hurt making the jump, but Teresa was smart. One day K.O. watched her jump from the lanai to the palm tree a few feet away, and then shinny backwards to the ground. Later, she reversed this and appeared in K.O.'s living room. After that, K.O. installed the pet door and didn't worry.

K.O. put on a pot of coffee and started bread toasting. Then she went to the lanai to assess the damage. The landscaping below her deck looked like a giant had run through picking up bushes and small trees and throwing them around. The tiled lanai was wet and slick so she got a towel and dried it. The lanai furniture was soaked too, but other than blotting the seats a bit, she let that go.

Raj wandered out next to her, looking slightly more awake and holding out a full coffee cup that matched his own.

"Thanks," K.O. said.

Raj nodded. "Some kine mess, yeah?"

"At least we don't have to clean it up. Homeowner's Association dues pay for that."

"Any leaks or anything?" he asked.

"Nothing obvious so far." K.O. headed back into the living room and plopped in her favorite recliner with the view of the mountains. Raj settled in the adjoining one and they both sipped until Teresa startled him by jumping onto the arm of his chair from behind.

"Whoa, little kitty." Raj held his cup aloft steadying the contents. Teresa delicately stepped into his lap and curled there purring.

"Well, somebody's got a fan," K.O. said. Teresa didn't really take to anyone except her. "I guess you been here long enough to be considered 'family.'"

"Nah. She got good taste." Raj gently petted her and the purring increased.

"Now you're trapped. You can't move. I made some toast. Guava jelly?"

"T'anks, eh. And more coffee." At his slightly imperious tone, K.O. raised her eye brows. "Please? I'm stuck," he added.

K.O. took his cup and headed into the kitchen. "I gotta call in; see if I need to be anywhere. I was supposed to be off today to watch you surf, but I bet no contest, today." She buttered toast and added an even layer of guava jelly to both their stacks of bread. Coffee refills and plates on a tray, she returned to the living room. Raj winced.

"You okay? Get hurt yesterday in those waves?" She handed him his cup and put his toast plate on the wide chair arm where he could reach it.

"No, I'm fine. It's just," he gasped, "her claws. She's really happy."

K.O. laughed. "Been there, brah. Got punctures to prove what a good cat mother I am. Want me to move her?"

"No, I'm good. She's fine. I wish a little less happy, you know?" They shared a smile.

"So, what's on for today?" K.O. asked.

"I want to see the waves." Typically winter surf was big on the North Shore anyway, but with a storm, it might be spectacular. K.O. loved the water, but wasn't much of a surfer. Her daredevil side came out when she had jumped off 'the rock' into Waimea Bay with her former clerk from Records, Selina. Although K.O. wasn't in Records anymore, she and Selina remained friends.

"Sounds good. I want to go, too. I want to see if there's damage to the property and to the highway on our way there," she added. "I have to call in and see if they need me."

"Go ahead. I'm not in a hurry. I know I slept a lot, but was kind of stressful, yeah?"

"I know. I could use a rest day, too. Maybe we go up and check it out and then grab some lunch. Maybe more than the shrimp truck?"

"Great! I thought you didn't have to fix the damage?"

"I do if it's the townhouse proper. Not the grounds. I want to see from the outside. Maybe trees fell, you know? My car!"

"What?"

"The parking lot. I can't see my car from here." K.O. tore into her room, robe and bedroom slippers flying and came out in record time in jeans, a tee shirt and rubber slippers.

"I'll come, too." Raj stood and put Teresa gently on the chair and followed K.O. out the front door. He slept in jams and a tee shirt so he was ready for anything. He didn't bother with flip flops like K.O. had.

They raced down the stairs into what looked like the aftermath of a hurricane. Iwa and Iniki had left similar paths of destruction to island residents and the lot was littered with palm fronds and torn bushes. K.O.'s lovely silver car was covered in leaves and small branches, but nothing more substantial. She kept her light bar in the trunk when not on duty, so it was safe, too.

"That's so lucky!" K.O. and Raj began removing the rubbish from on top and around the car. She glanced at the parking lot and didn't see any damage to vehicles worse than hers. No felled trees. They returned to the townhouse and began a walk around inspection. K.O.'s unit was on the end of the building, so only one neighbor next door and one below. As neighbors go, they were pretty quiet. She couldn't see any problems, but water damage might show up later. For now, however, it was a relief.

They trudged back inside and K.O. made a more substantial breakfast of eggs and rice for her, and for Raj, accompanied it with Portuguese sausage. As they ate, she called in to work.

She hung up the receiver. "Okay, we go!"

"Right on," Raj said around a mouthful of eggs and rice. "Pass the shoyu?"

K.O. handed over the soy sauce. "Want more? I can make some more eggs if you want. We gotta go to the store, today after. On the way home."

Raj nodded. "Okay. I'm getting full, so no need more eggs, Auntie. Thanks."

"I'm going to get ready and we can go, okay?" K.O. rose and put her dishes in the sink before heading to her bathroom to see if make-up could hide her stress. She looked in the mirror. Not so much.

She did the best she could and also packed a small bag with a change of clothes in case the weather got bad again. Out the lanai the sky wasn't very blue and the weather was predicted to be stormy off and on through the weekend. That was bad for the surf contests since they could surf in rain, but not if the waves went crazy.

When she came back to the living room, she found Raj had cleaned up from breakfast. Without even asking. Wow. He was growing up. Maybe she should ask for Alani's Papaya car today, too, and he could practice driving. Take his mind off surfing, maybe. This contest was huge and a big step in his career if he decided to pursue pro surfing. It was weird, she mused, to think of a fifteen year old boy with a 'career.'

The Papaya was a stick shift, so that should keep Raj busy. K.O. smiled remembering stick shift lessons in parking lots growing up in Seattle. Her parents had moved to Mercer Island after she'd become an adult and moved to Hawai'i.

She popped her head into his room to thank him and found the traitorous Teresa on *his* pillow. "Oh, I see how you are."

"What?" Raj asked from behind her.

"Her." K.O. pointed to the tabby curled tightly, almost upside down, sound asleep. Raj's laugh made her smile. What a great kid.

"Right. Ready to go?" he asked.

"Yup. I grabbed some extra clothes in case the weather gets bad while we're out. Forecast is iffy at best. Grab some stuff while I get snacks."

Raj complied and a few minutes later they were out the door and back on the road they had traveled yesterday.

Although the sky was not as dark, it was by no means sunny and clear. More rain lurked. The highway was fairly free of debris, but the sides of the road were filled with branches, leaves and glimpses of undefinable objects. Everything glistened and K.O. bet the sandy shoulders of the road were quicksand for motorists.

People moved about, clearing banana leaves, palm fronds and coconuts from yards and side streets. Soon they were past where the highway split and she drove the narrow, curvy waterfront lane they had traversed only yesterday. The damage was worse here so close to the ocean. She couldn't tell if the road was actually closer to the water than it had been, but it felt like it. Most of the land was rock and lava, so perhaps it hadn't been swept out to sea.

"I guess it's for the best we couldn't see the water last night, yeah?" K.O. asked Raj.

"I dunno. Sucks either way."

K.O. had to agree. The storm surge had receded to normal levels and the road was dry. She glanced over at the houses every now and again and thought she saw high water marks on some of them. She couldn't restrain a shudder. When they passed the beach parks, she saw they had been converted to temporary staging areas for downed trees and branches. Road crews dumped their loads and from the looks of the piles, they had been hard at work for hours. She stuck her head out the window and slowed.

"Hey, brah, da folks out here get electricity?" she hollered to a couple workers in orange vests.

"Nah, not yet. Should be soon though. You live out here?" *Here* was pronounced *hee-ya* in ultimate pidgin.

"Nah, town. Just goin' to check out da waves wit' my neph." K.O. amped up her pidgin to meet his. She pointed to Raj who obligingly smiled and waved. "Road okay to Sunset?"

"I heard it's open, but one lane, mebbeh?"

"T'anks, eh, brah. You take care. You guys doin' a great job." She rolled up her window and continued north on Kam Highway.

The pewter sea roiled with debris. They stopped at Turtle Bay resort for a quick peek at the ocean. And coffee. K.O. needed more coffee. Even with the car heater on, she was chilled.

"You like more coffee? I gotta get some." K.O. swung into the resort parking lot. Not many spaces open. The few North Shore hotels filled up as well as all vacation rentals for the surf contests.

"I'm hungry, too."

"I can't believe how much you eat. You want snack or meal?"

"Um, burger, maybe?"

"Okay. Let's go in. They got a restaurant that's good and should be quick." She made her way through the lobby, festively decorated for Christmas. A huge tree layered in ornaments centered the check-in area adjacent to a small coffee bar. Since they were getting food, she bypassed that to head to the restaurant with a view of the pool and grounds. It was close to the inlet and an ocean view, but most of that was obscured by landscaping.

A cute hostess seated them near the curving windows and asked what they'd like to drink.

"Coffee," they said together.

She set down menus and smiled. "You got it."

Mere seconds later a young man with a coffee pot swung by and filled their cups. "Water?" he asked.

"Sure. No ice, please," K.O. said.

"I'm going to get this island burger. Looks ono," Raj said.

"Me, too, only veggie burger style. Fries?"

"Of course."

"Of course."

A different young man came by to take their orders. Raj watched the dining room while K.O. had the garden view.

"Hey, Jet's here. And Aliki."

K.O. was not a big fan of Jet, but knew how important he was to Raj. "Who's Aliki?" She turned to see the back of Jet's head facing a local-looking man in his 30s. His hair had been bleached by the sun to orangey highlights. Crows' feet K.O. could see from here, told of hours squinting in the sun. He was muscular and fit with a wide nose and dark eyes.

"He's another alternate like me sponsored by Bad Boyz Beach. I tol' you about him."

K.O. didn't remember. "Probably, but tell me again."

"Hey, lots of the surfers are here." Raj's mouth stayed open. "The famous ones. Oh, my gosh."

K.O. turned and saw many young, fit men and women in the dining room. That surprised her a little; Turtle Bay was a pricey hotel.

"Surfers are staying here?" she asked.

"Well, yeah. Some of the big ones with awesome sponsors."

"So the sponsors pay for the hotels? I didn't know there was that kind of money involved. I

59

thought they only got that 'house' arrangement you mentioned."

"Where you been, Auntie?" Raj said with some exasperation. "I been telling you, there's big money in surfing. I know, I know . . ." he flapped his hands to forestall her comment, "not for everyone, just the top, but it's worth it. I might be good enough someday." His face, still young and round, leaned toward her over the table.

K.O. felt her heart swell. "I know you can do it, if it's what you want. I'll help you, you know that. That's why I put up with you." She thought she might cry so she tried a little humor. "It's even worse living with you now that my cat likes you better." She sipped her coffee to reset her tear ducts.

The moment was lost as two hot plates were set in front of them.

"Oh, man," Raj said, grabbing his burger and taking a bite.

"Thank you," K.O. said, as she reached for the ketchup.

"Anything else?" the waiter enquired.

"Dis is perfect," Raj said around his mouthful.

K.O. shook her head since she now had taken a bite. After swallowing she asked, "How much money are we talking? How much is enough to get a surfboard company to put up ten surfers at a five star hotel in Hawai'i?"

"Well, the Reef Hawai'ian Pro is like $100,000 in prize money."

"What?" K.O. choked on her French fry.
"You're kidding, right?"

"No ways, Auntie. There's lots of contests
and lots of money to make out there. That's why
we take chances sometimes. That can be the
difference between a good ride and a winning ride.
And that's just for the contests. I don't know what
the sponsors get. Prolly way more den dat. But the
real money is in endorsements. Like, if they want
you to sell sunglasses or shoes. Li' dat."

K.O. was about to comment when two
figures arrived at the table. She looked up and saw
Jet and Aliki. Hawai'ian men aren't usually
particularly tall, but both these guys were built. Not
fat, but all muscle, from years of waging war in the
surf. She knew that surfing was territorial and a lot
of fights started in the water and ended on the
beach. She'd taken enough reports to vet that for
herself. It was sometimes racial, sometimes it was
new surfers from other places not understanding the
way the surf world works in Hawai'i, and
sometimes it was 'my wave.'

"Hey, little man," Jet greeted Raj. K.O.
didn't like that demeaning nickname, but Raj
seemed to. He was the youngest on the BBB team.

"Hey, Jet. What are you doing here?" Raj
said.

"What *choo* doin' here?" Aliki said.

K.O. thought she detected a note of hostility,
but if so, his wide smile covered it well.

"We're going up to check the waves. Got
hungry." Raj remembered his manners, partly.
"Jet, my Auntie K.O. Auntie, my sponsor Jet."

"Yeah, we met." Jet stuck out his hand. "At the beach."

"Oh, yeah," Raj said.

K.O. shook the limp hand offered. Being a woman in a mostly men's profession, she was often greeted with less than enthusiastic handshakes, and this was pretty weak. Sometimes she thought they didn't want to 'hurt' her hand, but other times, like now, it felt like a decided insult.

"Dis da Auntie?" Aliki asked. "Whoa, man you made her like one witch or somet'ing. She hot, brah."

K.O. felt another insult, perhaps two, had been tossed her way. "No, worries. I can be a witch. Where my nephew is concerned. Just looking out for him, *brah*," she said in perfect English.

Raj had turned red and even Jet looked a little abashed at Aliki's comment. Probably because Jet *had* said it. Aliki looked at her speculatively, in that offensive way men looked at women, particularly tourists, or white women here, designed to throw them off or make them feel vulnerable. *Good luck, buddy,* she thought. *My gun's probably bigger than yours.* She gathered Raj hadn't mentioned her line of work. She decided to keep it to herself.

"You must be Aliki?" K.O. asked.

"Yeah, you heard of me?" Aliki began to puff up.

"No. It's that Raj said he qualified yesterday and that you were the other alternate." She decided not to push it and embarrass her nephew. She didn't add that Raj's score ranked higher than his, and perhaps elevated him above Aliki in the rankings.

She ignored Aliki and turned to Jet. "What are you boys up to today? The contest is cancelled, right?" Subtle emphasis on *boys*.

"Yeah, cancelled for today. I'm meeting with my team, you know, goal-setting and what not."

His English had improved remarkably.

"Isn't Raj part of the team? Didn't he qualify yesterday?" K.O. asked.

Jet fumbled a bit. "Yes, sure. I just hadn't gotten around to calling everyone yet."

"We don't have a schedule today. I'm happy for you to meet with him now." K.O. smiled widely, showing her cooperation.

It was almost comical the way Jet did an internal 180 from whatever was really on his mind, and whatever he had going with Aliki, and said, "Sounds great. Let me get my files and meet him here in the lobby in a few minutes?"

"Sure, we're almost done." K.O. slightly stressed the *we* part, since she was Raj's guardian in the islands and for the purposes of the contest. If Jet thought he was going to pull a fast one on her watch, well, get ready.

Aliki did not look pleased. As they moved off, she heard him say, "What's with that, brah? Dis my time. We got strategy, man."

K.O. was a little surprised he knew the word 'strategy,' but maybe he was a great actor; learning from his boss, Jet. K.O. didn't trust either of them as far as she could throw them.

"Sorry, Auntie. Aliki is so rude. I think he's scared. You know, he gettin' old."

"No excuse for bad manners. I think Jet is a businessman who wants the best from his assets, and you are one of those. That's understandable. You're up and coming and Aliki is on the way out. Now that you've told me about how much money is involved, I totally get it. Aliki might be dangerous. Stay away from him. All business meetings will go through me. I have power of attorney to sign contracts for you. We will talk everything through together, but if I smell a rat, I'm not signing anything."

Raj looked relieved. "I know. I'm glad."

K.O. paid the check and they moved to the lobby to wait. They stood by the *makai* windows that faced the sea.

"Still pretty rough out there," K.O. said.

"Yeah, but you know dere's guys surfing it right now."

"After our meeting, let's go look at the bay side and see who's out there before we go to Sunset."

"Good. Can we go to Haleiwa, too? I want to see the waves where the Hawai'ian Reef contest was."

"You were there!"

"I know, but not when da waves was crazy."

K.O. smiled down at him. But not by much. She realized how much taller he was this visit, nearly reaching her 5-7.

Jet managed to sneak up on them and clapped a hand on Raj's shoulder. "You ready to talk strategy, little man?"

"We sure are," K.O. said. She kept her face neutral, but was happy for the sour twist on Jet's mouth at being outmaneuvered. By a *gurl*.

"Okay, let's sit over here." Jet led the way to a lobby conversation area with two plush couches in an L shape and two ample armchairs completing a U. He slid a file folder on the coffee table.

"What's the plan?" Raj asked. "I'm ready."

"You sure are, little man. You did great yesterday and you placed higher in the rankings. You know, sorry about Aliki." He nodded to K.O. "He a little piss-off that a squirt ranks higher than him, you know."

K.O. had figured right. "Sure, no prob." She smiled, promising herself to take off more time if she needed to keep Raj safe. She wondered if Raj's parents, Maureen and Joe, realized the kind of money and risk involved. Joe had been a surfer when he was young, but hadn't pursued it much past high school. They might have been kept in the dark if the boy's naiveté and Jet's manipulation combined to short circuit Raj's dreams.

Jet turned his attention to Raj and opened the file. "Okay, here's the current rankings and what's going to happen the next day we back in the contest." He showed Raj a list with print too small for K.O. to read upside down from her position on the adjacent armchair.

"Am I going to surf?" Raj asked.

"Of course you are. Everyone does. If someone gets disqualified, then you have to have your stats already."

Raj's face showed he had not realized that. K.O. knew he might not have paid attention at some briefing or another, whatever they called it in surfing. He was probably too excited. Not to excuse Jet completely, but it was possible. It sounded a little like a jury pool. The alternate jurors have to sit through the whole case from the get-go, lucky them, in case a juror can't or doesn't serve out the case. The alternates already have to have heard all the testimony in order to render a verdict.

"What about Aliki?" Raj asked.

"Well, sure, he's in, too. What did you think?"

"Why's he so mad?"

"You so young. I think you higher than him at the same age, and you know he's getting older. This might be his last year."

"Oh."

"Okay, so here's your competition. You know how we watch all those videos of everyone's rides?" Raj nodded. "It's so we can see how you can get bettah, and who you gotta watch out for. Okay, dis guy, Myles Freeh from California. He gonna be a problem. He young like you, not as young, but kinda star beach boy and doing good. He could boot you out early." He poked a strong finger at another name K.O. couldn't read. "Dis guy, Tai Phillips from Australia, he tops and he get experience, you know?"

66

"How can I prep for all that? Too much can happen," Raj mumbled. K.O wondered the same thing.

"A lot depends on the wave you choose. That's almost the only control you have. And that depends on the waves in the set and where you are in the time on the heat."

"So what do we do?" K.O. asked. Now she was a *we,* with Raj and Jet.

"I like him to watch some videos of the competition. I got a video player in my room and I have the team watch. I brought more footage from yesterday along with some other days."

"Of themselves? Or the other guys," K.O. asked. "What room?" Her response was a little delayed but her alarm went off at 'my room.'

"Both. And I get a room here so we can have meetings and watch the footage. It's better than at the house. Too noisy. It's important to have them watch. I brought a VCR I can hook up to the TV in the room."

K.O. must have showed concern because he added, "I have the only key, and I call the meetings. It's not a clubhouse, it's business."

K.O. tried to look like she was reassured. It sounded good, but she knew a lot of ways to get into a hotel room—once one guy was in, he opened the door for the others was the first that came to mind. She also didn't like it that Raj was so much younger than everyone else. Adult men in an unsupervised hotel room was a recipe for disaster and she would make sure Raj took no part. She was relieved that Mau and Joe had said absolutely NO to

Raj's initial query that he stay with the team at the hotel. *Or now at a remote house*, she thought to herself.

"Let me know when you need Raj to watch footage and I'll be happy to drive him up."

Both Raj and Jet looked less than thrilled. Neither had a choice. K.O. sat back in her plush chair while they continued to discuss tubes and backs and fronts and weight distribution, statistics and many things K.O. knew nothing about. Her limited surfing experience had ended in few rides, many falls, and an occasional injury. Mostly not serious, but one bad fall in shallow water had landed her straight on her head. That had been the end of her surfing career.

Jet did seem like he knew was he was talking about. He *should* have his surfers best interests at heart, but K.O. couldn't help thinking she was missing something. Maybe she should start paying more attention to the nuts and bolts of the sport and less attention to the fit forms of the athletes themselves. Well, she wasn't blind, was she? Her thoughts drifted to her Hawai'ian boyfriend, Alani, who did surf—not professionally—and coincidentally, filled out his jams and tee shirts quite nicely.

She brought her brain back to earth as Raj and Jet stood to shake hands.

"We'll schedule some video time tomorrow, okay?" Jet said.

"Okay!" Raj was on board.

Jet turned and stuck out his hand. K.O. was surprised to receive a decent shake. Hmm. Food for thought. He was a man of contrasts. Not always a bad sign, but she had a vibe that he was up to something.

Chapter 6

K.O. could tell Raj was on a surf-high after the meeting with Jet. They left the lobby and headed out past the pool to view the little bay. Surfers had a heck of a paddle from the shore to the break, and K.O. wondered why they didn't start from the edge of the bay. Maybe it was hotel property and the uppity clients didn't want to see surfers trudging through the ti leaves and plumeria trees with their boards and unsightly sandy feet.

The bay was rough. A few surfers dotted the break line and caught the occasional decent curl. Didn't seem worth it to K.O., but what did she know? She'd rather sit at the Elks lodge with a beverage and watch Alani and the other surfers try their luck in Waikiki.

"Okay, we go," Raj pronounced after thoroughly gauging the water. K.O. dutifully followed him back to the parking lot. The sky looked about the same so they continued on the highway to Pipeline to see what was up with the contest.

"It looks like the clean-up crews haven't made it this far," Raj observed. This section highway was noticeably more strewn with foliage, although by comparison the Turtle Bay grounds were immaculate.

"Road looks dry, though. We can make it." K.O. kept her speed down and shortly they reached Ehukai Beach and searched for a place to park along the highway. Cars and trucks nosed into the shrubbery as far as the eye could see. A few intrepid souls parked at Sunset Beach Elementary, but K.O. didn't want to play her HPD card here. She didn't have any professional friends on the North Shore. Finally a tiny space was possible, if they didn't really want to open their doors. K.O. parked so Raj's door was close to the next car. He wiggled past the steering wheel to exit the driver's side. They cut through the bushes to the walking path, then through to the park where the food trucks sat. Past those, the beach was almost unrecognizable. The shape of the berms had changed overnight, and the rise that K.O. had watched from yesterday had moved back almost to the property lines. She wondered what it looked like under water. The angle of the beach under the waves greatly affected the waves themselves. Pipeline was shallow over a reef necessitating careful if fast, decisions. The stretch itself was about two miles long, and it offered some of the best winter surf anywhere in the world.

Raj bobbed his head in the 'hey' greeting known throughout the islands, to a few folks watching the waves. For such crowded parking, K.O. sure didn't see them on the sand.

"Let's go see if anyone's at the stand," Raj said. He headed toward the multi-story judging area so she followed. It looked a little windblown, but that it was standing at all surprised K.O. Organizers threw that thing up in record time and she wondered that it hadn't blown over like the pili grass house in the story of *The 3 Little Pua'a and the Magic Shark*, which was the Hawai'ian version of the three little pigs story she had read to Raj and Justine.

Raj was at the window talking to someone— well, listening—by the time she made her way through the sand to him. She leaned in.

"I dunno, brah," said the tanned man with dreadlocks. "I heard one storm coming in tonight, so we kinda wait and see fo' tomorrow."

"K den. Wassup today? Anyt'ing?"

"Nah. Guys is just having fun, you know?"

Raj's smile said he did know, but in K.O.'s opinion, that was more like insanity. She hadn't realized how big the surf was when they'd first arrived. Now, the waves were filled with figures sailing down on tiny boards, she tried to do the math. If each figure is about six feet tall . . . no good.

"How big is the surf?" she asked dreadlocks.

"About twenny, twenny-five." He scratched in between some hair rolls with a pencil. "I seen bigger."

Distracted by what might be in his hair, she thought she heard wrong.

"Twenty-five feet high?"

He squinted toward the sea, then picked up some binoculars. "Yeah, around that. Some sets is biggah, you know? But mostly that. We had some monsters when the waves was really goin' yesterday."

K.O. remembered the terrifying drive. "People surfed in that?"

"Oh, yeah. Da crazy guys."

K.O. was relieved to hear that *something* was considered crazy in the surfing world. She knew during hurricane watches and tidal wave alerts, lots of people rushed to get in the water while she rushed to higher ground. Jeez.

"Coupla guys almost bought it. Lotsa trees in da watah and dey no can see 'um good." He laughed at the memory. "Dey miss, so hey, dey stay in da contest, right?"

"Wow," Raj exhaled the word.

K.O. poked him. "No ways, buddy. Not on your life."

"When I'm 21."

"When you're 80 and I'm dead," K.O. said.

A half smile lit Raj's face. He turned his attention back to the stand. "So, am I in the lineup for the next day we can compete?"

"You said Dela Cruz, right?" Raj nodded. "Yeah, you here. You got good scores, brah. Bettah den me my first time."

"Did you get to compete?"

"Nah. Never needed me as alternate. But, hey, watch and learn brah, watch and learn."

"T'anks, eh?" Raj did a complicated hand-slapping shaking thing with him as he took his leave. It looked comical to K.O., but she held her tongue. She loved to rib him, but some things, she knew, were sacred.

"So, Auntie, if I can borrow a board, you t'ink—"

"No way. Look out there. You can see stuff in the waves."

They turned to study the water and several dark shapes swept up in the curl. As the wave broke, a small row boat section launched upward, a broken mast, and a palm tree piece flew over the foam.

"Okay. I get 'um," Raj said glumly.

"Hey, you get plenny time fo' break yo' head," K.O. said in her best pidgin.

Raj rolled his eyes. "I guess."

"Tell you what, we'll come back tomorrow unless it's raining or the storm tonight makes it worse, okay?" A small nod. "Let's check out Haleiwa and get some lunch."

He tried not to pout and K.O. appreciated the effort. He was growing up.

Back in the car, they continued toward one of the cutest little beach towns—sort of stuck in the 1950's with boardwalks instead of sidewalks, and a business district about two blocks long. A little longer if you counted the gentrifying at the western end with a grocery store, pizza place and a bank. And a dozen or so surf-related stores. One of just about everything a person would need to live here.

Or at least vacation here. K.O. loved it, but knew it was too small for her.

"Let's eat first then hunt for surf, okay?" she asked.

"Sounds good. Pizza?"

"Anything you want. Maybe Matusmoto's shave ice after?"

"Now you talking!" Raj was definitely cheered up.

After they shared a pizza, pepperoni on his half, and pineapple and green pepper on hers, they drove back to the tiny shave ice stand. They ordered rainbow ice with both adzuki beans and vanilla ice cream in the bottoms of the cones and sat on one of the wooden benches outside. They tried to eat it faster than it could melt. A tough job since even in winter, the weather was warm and the storm had brought additional humidity. Plus, they were already stuffed from the pizza.

"Argh," Raj said as he slid down the bench to ease his stomach.

"Fo' real, argh," K.O. repeated. "Ready to go?"

"Yeah." Raj lurched up unsteadily.

"We could walk. Not too far. Right there." She pointed with her thumb over her shoulder through the store. As the crow flies, she was pretty accurate, but she didn't know if the neighbors would appreciate them taking the direct approach through private homes or yards.

"You're kiddin', right?" Raj asked.

"Yeah, I am. Less go."

They made it back to the car and she drove the few blocks to Ali'i Beach Park where the Hawai'ian Reef contest was held.

Since the contest was over, only locals and a few off-the-path tourists utilized the park. Several families had staked out picnic tables under shade structures and some big parties looked to be in the making.

K.O. easily found a spot in the big lot and they waddled slowly toward the crest of grass to the beach.

"I so full," K.O. slowed even more on the slight incline.

"Me, too. Come on, Auntie. You can do it." Raj grabbed her hand to tow her and she made a show of resisting, but she was touched by his thoughtfulness. Since he got to his teens he was significantly less affectionate beyond the obligatory hug at arrival and departure.

They reached the sand and took in the view. A large open area of water, an entrance to a small port for fishing boats nearby, and a wide expanse of open beach. The waves were decent in K.O.'s estimation, and the number of surfers supported her assessment.

Raj froze as he watched, a slight grin lifting his face into something like his toddler looks. K.O. felt a pang of unwanted nostalgia.

"Rather surf here tomorrow or Pipeline?" She asked to distract herself.

Raj plopped into the sand right where he was. "Pipeline," he mumbled. "Gotta practice on site as much as I can."

"True. Maybe the storm changed the break, you know?" K.O. said.

"Mebbe. Ho!" Raj slapped the sand. "You see that?"

"No, what did I miss?"

"Dat guy, he shoot the curl, den flip ovah da back side . . . so awesome!"

"How big the wave? I mean, why was it more awesome?"

"Auntie, you gotta watch. Da wave was big, but was rough! And he hung it, man. Didn't lose it even at the end. Righteous!"

Righteous? Was that a surf word now? "Who is it? You know this guy?"

"I don't know. Prolly not from the contests. Everybody is practicing back at Pipeline."

Did he emphasize that a little too much? K.O. thought. "We should go since you're not surfing today, anyway." She emphasized that a little. Ha.

He looked at her sideways, picking up on that. They had always had a connection that way. "Fine." He smiled. "When you gonna let me practice driving? You said."

"Workin' da angles, huh brah? Guilting me?"

"Nah, but you did say."

"Okay, lemme call Alani." She left him on the beach and headed to the pay phone at the edge of the lot. "Maybe I should get one of those cell phones," she mused. "Big as a brick, but maybe more convenient." Half the time pay phones didn't work anyway.

Her boyfriend was a wood-carver; an artisan who made gorgeous bowls and sculptures in his home studio. He almost always answered his phone unless he was deep into creative-mode. No answer, but his machine picked up.

"Hey, it's me. Just wanted to know if I could borrow the Papaya for some lessons for Raj. I mentioned it when he was coming for the contest, but he's a little antsy right now. The weather has made the surf bad for a while, so I hoped I could distract him with driving. We're at Ali'i Beach now but heading home. Leave me a message and I'll bring him to get the car. Thanks."

She headed back to the beach but Raj was already coming her way. "Hey, Alani didn't answer but I left a message. Let's go back home. We gotta do food shopping at Times' and then maybe Alani will have called. We can get the car after that if you want."

"Great!" Raj was fully recovered from whatever surf-induced funk he'd been in.

The road conditions improved as they drove. The work crews had made good progress and they whipped into the Times' Supermarket parking lot without a single death scare.

They joked their way through the store, buying equal amounts of healthy choices and junk food. For a kid, Raj really loved fruits and veggies. They barbequed on her lanai a lot when he visited. They sat and talked for hours around meals and snacks. She felt fortunate because she doubted his parents got that much attention. Between school and surfing, preparing for contests or travel, she didn't think that left much time for chatting. His sister, Justine, older by two years and getting ready to graduate high school, was giving her parents a run for their money, according to K.O.'s phone calls with Maureen; mostly about unsuitable boys, a bit about letting her grades slip and thinking her job at Seattle's Best Coffee was 'lame,' they had their hands full.

K.O. could offer no reassurance because she had been far from an angel in her teen years. She hoped Maureen hadn't found out about a lot of it, or she'd never sleep again. K.O. still enjoyed going out with friends, but she was a lot older now. *I should know better by now*, she smiled to herself.

Raj helped bring all the groceries upstairs and began to put them away.

"I'm going to check and see if Alani left a message," K.O. said. "Leave out what you want for dinner and we'll start to prep that."

Alani was happy to let Raj drive the Papaya. As he said, "It can't get any worse-looking, even if he rolls it!"

"Is that what he thinks?" Raj overheard the message and yelled from the kitchen.

"He's kidding. Okay, wanna go get it and we'll have a practice?"

"You bet! Should I leave this stuff out?" he indicated the dinner items.

"Salad stuff is fine unless you want it cold, but you better put away the shoyu chicken if you don't want Teresa to get it. Her favorite thing in the world is chicken."

"I know. Okay." He replaced items in the refrigerator. "I marinated the chicken so it should be ready when we get back."

"What about me?" Raj knew she was a vegetarian, but hadn't always been. She had taught him a lot of 'island' recipes like shoyu chicken, kal bi beef, and loco moco breakfast. He made sure she had options, too, when he shopped or cooked by himself.

"What about you? We got salad." His eyes twinkled so she knew there was more.

"Fine, no Papaya car." She folded her arms.

"Got you. Shoyu tofu. Marinating in a separate bowl."

"I knew there was something. Thanks."

K.O. had even splurged on a two-part grill, one for meat and one for her options.

"Ready?" she asked. "Let's go." She checked that Teresa had kibble and water and grabbed her keys. They slapped down the stairs to the car in companionable silence.

Alani lived a few miles away, toward the main part of Kaneohe, in a cute little duplex. Two houses and the connecting walls were the two garages. His neighbor was elderly Mr. Lim, who watched out for Alani's place when he had to travel. Mr. Lim's philosophy was, "You never know." K.O. agreed, but it was interesting for her to imagine 80 year old Mr. Lim doing anything besides punch in 911. He was notorious for not liking the kids in the neighborhood (anyone under fifty) and would shout "Get off my lawn!" at them, even if they were not on it. Inexplicably he had taken a shine to Alani, infant that he was in his mid-thirties.

The Papaya was parked on the street, keys under the mat since he wouldn't be home, as his message indicated. She parked the Crown Vic behind it and they hopped in. The Papaya was unlocked, because, well, it couldn't be locked. It was worse than she remembered. The front seats relaxed back, and the back seat sprang forward as if leaning toward the driver. Padding? Nope, but a couple old beach towels helped prevent impalement from the seat innards. K.O. rummaged in the back for another towel to fill the space between the seat back and the person trying to sit up.

"Hmmm. You gotta be able to see, Raj." K.O. sighed, hands on her hips. "Try wait." She dug around in her trunk for another towel for the passenger's side. She rolled that up and sat, testing.

"I gotta be able to see too. Or maybe I don't want to?" She smiled. "Hop in. Let's see what this baby can do."

"I'll be happy if this 'baby' starts." Raj gingerly sat in the driver's seat and wriggled. No doubt arranging *okole* and springs into a more accommodating arrangement.

"Okay, you gotta check your mirrors and seat." K.O. put on her seatbelt. Raj did the same and she was relieved to see they looked in good shape.

Raj attempted to adjust his side mirror to no avail. No mirror on her side at all. The rearview moved in millimeters. He strained to see behind him, sitting up tall.

"You sure dis legal, Auntie?" For the first time, Raj looked a little less thrilled about driving.

"Well, it's registered and passed the safety check. Let's give it a go. If you no like, we go home." Raj sat unmoving. "You want me to drive it first? I'm sure it's okay." K.O. reverted to standard English to reassure him. "Alani knew you were going to drive it, so it's fine. I was just kidding with you." Raj still made no move to start it. "I'm sorry."

"It's not that. I, uh, nevah drove a stick before."

"Oh!" A big gush of relief. "No problem. You can't hurt this transmission so no worries."

K.O. walked him through the basics with the engine off. She made sure they were secured in their scary seats and then Raj made inching progress down the residential block in first. He slid into second, but got lost and stalled heading to third.

K.O. thought it would be alarming having a teenager drive, and she with the responsibility of it. Maureen had made it sound like defusing a bomb, like Raj would go 'off' at any second and do donuts and 180s or race away at 100mph. Raj listened to everything she said and did his best to follow directions. She stayed calm and relaxed and found the whole process strangely rewarding.

"Okay. Wanna take a break?" she asked fifteen minutes later when he hadn't stalled for three blocks.

"Not really. I feel like I'm getting it. Sort of." Raj smiled at her, a light mist of sweat on his upper lip. He wiped his hands on his jams and left damp streaks.

"I know, it's hard, but you doin' good. I think we should take a break so I'll give you some directions to follow like the driver's test guy, 'kay?"

"Okay."

She guided him to Zippy's Restaurant and he laughed when he saw where she was headed. He had looked nervous when she'd directed he turn onto the faster paced Kam highway, but he stayed in the right lane. Lots of traffic lights to slow the flow, and he was clearly pleased with his success and imminent reward.

"All right. Plate lunch, yeah?" he confirmed.

"I think you deserve it. Gotta keep those calories up if you gonna surf tomorrow."

They spent an hour relaxing, eating, and drinking milk shakes which were dessert as far as K.O. was concerned. Raj had done a great job and she couldn't reach out and hug him like when he was little. Zippy's was a teenager's reward for a job well done.

"Still feel like driving or you want a break?" she asked when they'd finished.

"I can make it back to Alani's, no problem. I can't drive your car, so all the practice I can get is great. Thanks for this."

"I'm happy it worked out. We'll do it again, okay?" Raj nodded. "Do you remember how to get back?" He shook his head as enthusiastically as he'd nodded and she burst out laughing. He'd always been able to make her laugh, ever since he was a baby.

"You one rascal. Okay, here we go." She
gave directions and on the way back he didn't stall
at all, but shifted smoothly. He drove cautiously like
all new drivers, but she let it go. She did remind
him to stay in his own lane and not to swing wide
on turns. She remembered how hard it was to feel
the boundaries of a new vehicle. Her Crown Vic
was enormous compared to her previous cars and
for a month she parked in two spots everywhere
because she didn't know how wide or long it was.

The evening passed peacefully and restfully
with second dinners of shoyu chicken and tofu.
Only one old movie and they were both ready to hit
the sack. Big day tomorrow. K.O. wasn't sure if
she was ready to tackle Jet and his attitude. But
she'd promised to take care of Raj, and she
promised Raj she'd get him to any 'strategy'
sessions and meetings.

Chapter 7

The next morning K.O. woke to hear Raj on the phone. It was unusual that he got up before her. She staggered to the coffee pot and bless him, he'd started it and enough filled the carafe to pour a cup. She doctored it with creamer and sweetener and took her first gratifying sip.

The mumbled conversation from Raj's room stopped as she plopped into her recliner to enjoy the mountain view. His door opened and he shuffled out followed by Teresa.

"Thanks for starting the coffee. I left you a drop."

"No prob." She heard a mug hit the counter and his own doctoring ensue. Cream and lots of sugar, she knew. He joined her in the other recliner and Teresa hopped up on the arm of his.

"Traitor," K.O. told her. Teresa lifted a paw and licked an imaginary hair into place.   Before K.O. could ask, Raj said, "That was Jet. He said we have a meeting at ten at the hotel. We can go, right?"

"Sure. Is this the strategy meeting?"

"Yeah. He, wants to discuss my career, he said." Raj looked very young as he said this. K.O. studied him over the rim of her cup.

"Will there be others from the team there?"

"Yeah. We gonna watch video of the last couple days. Not as much since the weather been bad, but he wants us each to . . . uh," Raj fished for a word.

"Evaluate?"

"Nah, but like that. Critique!" he managed after more coffee. "Critique our own rides and then we look at each other's and do the same."

"You look funny. What's wrong?"

"It feels funny. I'm the youngest and newest on the team and Aliki's already piss off at me and I'm going to give advice? "

"Everyone has eyes. Everyone has something to offer."

"Auntie, dis is surfing, not a business meeting. I say one t'ing wrong and I get beat up out there. Or worse."

That hadn't occurred to K.O. *I guess I did believe Jet when he said he had Raj's interests at heart.* She knew the feeling. It had happened before in her job. *It feels like a set up. But why? What would he gain from getting everyone mad at Raj?* Raj could be his next big money maker. It didn't make sense from an investment perspective.

"What do you want to do?"

He looked so down. "I'll figure something out. Let's go."

"Aren't you hungry? You're always hungry."

"Not really."

"It's early. You can't function at a strategy meeting, have career planning and then practice rides on only coffee."

"You sound like my mom."

"Well, I am *in loco parentis,* buddy."

"Wha . . .?"

"Latin. In place of the parent. Your school is that when you're there, too. So don't get cocky. You have to eat, so it's a matter of what you want."

He stroked Teresa while he thought. Her rumbling purr reached K.O. Cat therapy always worked.

"Manapua."

"For breakfast?"

"Yup, manapua. Now I'm hungry. How long it gon' take you to get beautiful, li' dat?" His spirits had risen.

"Not long. I so beautiful, I don't need much." K.O. finished her coffee. "But you, you're a mess. Get your bestest jams and purtiest tee shirt and let's hit the road. Your board okay at the team house? We go to the hotel first, right? Then get your board before practice?"

"Yup yup yup." He jumped up, startling Teresa. He headed to his room and she accepted the warm spot on the chair in exchange for his rudeness.

Dressed and out the door, it wasn't long before K.O. pulled into a disreputable looking alley.

"We breakin' in someplace, or what?" he asked when they stopped in front of a grimy door bordered by even grimier dumpsters.

"No. Your wish is my command, my prince." She opened the alley door and they stepped into a kitchen already bustling and filled with delicious smells. "Ni hao," she called.

"Ni hao," a woman answered and came out of the steam. They hugged.

"Ellie, dis my nephew, Raj. Raj, dis Ellie. Best Chinese restaurant on da island."

"Howzit," Raj said.

"I good, I good," Ellie said. She turned to K.O. "He cute, you right!"

Raj blushed while K.O. laughed and said, "So, he want manapua for breakfast. Only one place to go, yeah?"

"A course!" Ellie led them to a rack stacked with cooling manapua. Sweet white buns filled with barbequed, seasoned pork.

"Oh, my gosh!" Raj said. "Smells so *ono*."

"Used to be my favorite too, 'til I became a vegetable," K.O. said.

"Yeah, but you did me a favor, girl," Ellie said. "You not da only veg. I got a huge business from you turning against my food." K.O. laughed and Ellie continued. "When your Auntie tell me she no eat meat anymoah, I wondered about dat. So I start a whole line of veggie food and you know what?"

Raj shook his head, gamely trying to focus on the story but his eyes kept flicking to the sweet buns.

"I make a ton of money off those vegetables!"

"Don't let her fool you," K.O. said and led them to the dining room. Resembling a cafeteria with Chinese decor rather than a glitzy Chinese restaurant in Waikiki, she continued. "This place is jammed every night. Her husband Daniel, the chef, does amazing things with vegetables and tofu and wheat gluten you would not believe. It's one of the few vegetarian friendly Chinese places anywhere in the state. And it's the best. Of course."

Ellie beamed and handed Raj a bun. "Heah, before you like die."

Raj peeled off the little paper square on the bottom and took a huge bite mumbling *mahalo* through it. Ellie laughed. "I bettah get you folks some to go. I got a new one for you to try," she said to K.O. "plus your favorites."

Ellie headed back to the kitchen while Raj swallowed his mound of dough. "How come you never tol' me about this place? Or took me here?" he accused.

"I like to pace myself. Gotta have new things for da neph when he visit. Mo' bettah?"

"Oh, yeah. Thanks. I good now. I can face those guys." He marched back through the kitchen and she followed. Through the steam she saw him hug Ellie. Wow. He must really like those buns. *My little boy is growing up*, she thought. *But he's still not going to that meeting alone.*

She hugged Ellie too, and hollered to the rest of the kitchen staff, "Mahalo!"

The drive north was glorious, but it was also calm. Ellie's manapua had worked some magic and

Raj relaxed in his seat, glancing out the window occasionally, content with his thoughts.

K.O. not so much. Ellie's new bun was magically delicious, but she ran scenarios of Jet's meeting and possible motives through her head the whole way.

At the hotel, she had to park at the far side of the large lot. Damp asphalt and heavy plumeria perfume indicated a recent shower. They walked carefully, on the lookout for tourist driven golf carts. Sure enough, one whipped around an aisle of parked cars and K.O. and Raj jumped into the space between two cars to avoid collision.

"Whoa!" K.O. said as Raj said a more profane version. She didn't give him stink eye for it since she was thinking the same.

They continued between the rows of cars even more cautiously without talking. They wanted all faculties attuned for the next one. Those golf carts were stealthy, being electric. They heard raised voices at the same time.

"All we need is a domestic," mumbled K.O. Some of her worse calls were 'domestic,' meaning a family fight where even the person she was called to protect sometimes turned against her in favor of the abuser.

They continued, and K.O. tried to hear where the heated debate was coming from so she could avoid it. However, the packed lot made sound bounce around under the low-hanging cloud cover.

"Hey, das dat guy from Cali," whispered Raj.

"Who?"

"Myles Freeh. He really good. He's a favorite this year along with Buddy Soarez and Tai Phillips."

"I can't see who he's arguing with, can you?"

"I see da back of his head." Raj scooted closer duck-walking between cars.

K.O.'s duck-walking days were long over so she said, "Be careful!" She squatted to wait for him.

He returned, breathless. "Aliki Gomes! Das who he beef wit'."

"About what? Could you hear?"

"Sounded like Aliki dropped in on one noddah wave. Man, you cut off a guy like Myles Freeh, you in for it. Dey look like dey's ready to go, right heah!" Raj's eyes were bright with excitement.

K.O. wasn't on duty, and didn't want to get in between two large, muscular young men set on pummeling each other in the parking lot. She would not be able to protect Raj, and it wasn't her business. "Let's go."

"What? It's just getting good." Raj popped his head above the hood of a Toyota Corolla.

"No. We're not getting involved. If they want to fight, let them. You can tell Jet at the meeting." She checked her watch. "We gotta go or you'll be late."

"Shoots," he mumbled but complied.

They made their way to the lobby, Raj craning his neck to catch any action. "They coming," he said, dejected. "I don't t'ink dey even t'rew one punch."

"Don't sound so bummed about it. Somebody could have gotten hurt."

"Yeah, but maybe knock down some competition, yeah?"

"Raj! Really?" She turned to him and his eyes danced. "Babooze," she said and gently pushed him back a step.

"Anyway, if dey gon' fight, dey gon' fight sometime."

"Wow, you're like psychic now?"

"Auntie, come on. You know dat. People gon' beef if dey want to, and if dey stuck wit' each othah too much."

K.O. pushed the elevator button. "True. Okay, focus. Do you have a plan?"

"A plan for what?"

"Yeah, me neither. I'm staying in the meeting, though, so get that through your head."

"I know." His voice was petulant, but a sideways glance told K.O. he was a bit relieved. They were both way out of their depth here, but at least she was an adult. And a cynical one at that. Too bad she didn't know anyone in the pro surf world to bounce ideas off. She could use some advice. Alani had never gone pro but maybe he knew someone? She made a mental note as they headed down the hall.

The room door was propped open and a jumble of voices met them.

"Hey, you made it," Jet bro-hugged Raj and fake smiled at K.O. His smile didn't reach his eyes,

92

but he covered well. Quick introductions to several other young men which K.O. immediately forgot.

A shuffle at the door and Aliki came in and sat.

"Nice of you to show up," Jet said.

"Sorry, eh. Hadda do something." Aliki kept his head down.

K.O. tried to see if he had a bruise or cut but couldn't.

Jet talked them through the footage of the last couple days and the surfers hollered and cat called. To K.O., one ride didn't look all that different from another, but she paid attention and finally noticed the subtleties of waves and performance. Not before it was pointed out, of course, but at least she was 'getting it.' Then Jet showed footage of other team's surfers. Myles Freeh caught and hung onto anything he chose. Tai Phillips from Australia surfed like Spiderman, stuck to his board, defying gravity on the wave's face. Buddy Soarez, from Hawai'i but sponsored by Vans, was almost as good on those comparison rides.

She caught Raj's eye and knew they silently agreed they were probably looking at the top three right there. Not much chance for the BBB team and the likelihood of either Aliki or Raj making the cut were slim. She also noticed Raj looked relieved. Frankly, she was too.

Aliki's dark gaze intercepted the exchange. Besides his glare, she saw he had no facial marks. The fight hadn't escalated. Yet.

She smiled at him. They both knew his taped rides didn't showcase much of anything. Raj's super ride of yesterday was up with the top three guys, but that was a one-off. However, Aliki's closed fists and clenched jaw told her he was definitely angry and the parking lot action said he was not above taking it to a physical level. Maybe he had dropped in on purpose. He didn't smile back, but nodded in concession to her attempt at friendliness.

K.O.'s attention wandered and she observed the rest of the group. A guy with glasses, didn't look like a surfer, who hovered in the background with a pad and pen. The other guys looked like athletes. Nothing remarkable about them except they wore brightly colored sports shoes. Neon in fact, and each had a different color. Hmm, everyone wore a pair except Raj. What was up with that? She was sure she saw the BBB logo along the side. Maybe his pair was coming. Or it was another slight, to further separate and intimidate him.

Whether it was Jet's compassion or disorganization, he sent the guys off without having Raj critique another teammate's performance.

"Raj, come to the table. And Auntie of course," Jet added. "Time to talk individual strategy and your future here with BBB." Jet grinned widely and it reminded K.O. of the Cheshire cat. Not a comforting look.

The meeting was boring for K.O. and she knew most of it was over Raj's head. He was just a kid, but Jet threw in enough buzz words and carrots like, "prize money" and "meeting your potential" and "long term future with BBB" that Raj was drooling by the end, sure he was going to be the next world famous Kelly Slater. She also felt Jet changed his speech for her benefit. Not sure why or how, but she had learned to trust her gut in these matters.

"Okay!" Jet clapped his hands and stood. "Enough talk. We got practice runs to make."

"Great!" Raj jumped up, too. "See you there."

K.O. stood more slowly, thinking. "I have a question. What would happen if someone you sponsor dropped out? Who would be the one to fill in? Aliki or Raj?"

Jet froze for a millisecond. "Well, that depends on several factors. The current rides primarily. Best scores."

"So, it wouldn't automatically go to Aliki since he's been with you so long?" She didn't say 'older' but they both knew what she meant.

"Not necessarily. He does have seniority on the team, but it's really about the best rides."

"What about sportsmanship?"

"What do you mean?"

"Does your team policy address sportsmanship? I didn't see anything about that in the contract for Raj. I saw that he's not supposed to be convicted of a felony, but everything else seems wide open."

Jet was silent. K.O. smelled the smoke as his brain whirled like a hamster wheel while he thought. "That's a great idea. A sportsmanship clause. I wish I'd thought of it. After this big contest is over, I'll bring it to the board of trustees for discussion."

"Great." K.O. knew that was a non-answer, but the best she would get. This meant, nothing. And what board? She hadn't thought of it before, but it was a company, didn't it have to have a board? And who was on it?

"See you at the Pipe." Jet walked her out the door and closed it.

Raj danced impatiently at the elevator. "Come on, Auntie! Gotta get my stick. Let's go!"

The fifteen minute drive to the house at Pipeline was about a week long with Raj giving a running commentary on his future, his surfing, surfing in general, the lack of haste with which K.O. was driving, and the ocean he could see periodically from his window. If she squinted, she imagined he was a golden retriever hanging his head out, ears flapping and endlessly barking. That image made her smile and not push him out of the moving car.

Neither of them had been to the team house before, so they did a little loop around looking. Street names were buried in foliage while cars, bikes, and pedestrians were a constant hazard. K.O. had to watch her driving so that left Raj to look for addresses and complain how much surf time this was taking.

Again, she didn't push him out to walk on his own, but suggested he roll down his window and ask someone who looked local.

Mission accomplished. They found the house with no visible address, but the wrought iron turtle embossed gate was the landmark. No available parking of course. K.O. squished the Crown Vic parallel to the skinny road next to the dry stone wall bounding the property and prayed no one scraped the side. The department wouldn't cover repairs due to her unwise parking decisions while off-duty.

Raj had to slide out the driver's side once again and he wisely didn't complain but merely opened the turtle gate and ran up the walk. K.O. locked up and followed. Even inside the gate, the house was barely visible. Only a second story lanai rail peeked out of the trees and she saw a roofline a bit higher. The entire property was fenced or rather, walled, and dense jungle made visibility impossible. She stepped carefully on the rough stone walk to the open front door. The house was eerily silent. She couldn't even hear Raj thundering around looking for his board.

"Raj? Where are you?" She navigated a cluttered hall to an open-concept living room kitchen area. The obligatory Hawai'ian kitsch that was in nearly every rental had made it here. Floral upholstery on all bamboo furnishings, crossed canoe paddles on the living room wall, a war club in a case—the shark's teeth edging the wooden leaf-shape a sobering reminder of the warlike culture.

The tenants had made their presence known. Every inch was covered in surf related items. The mountain of slippers at the front door should have been a clue, but she wondered how many people lived here. Only three members on this tiny upstart company team, plus a house chaperone and two alternate surfers, one of whom wasn't staying here.

Assume Jet stayed here sometimes, and groupies . . . her thoughts stopped here, doubly glad she had nixed Raj's wish to stay at the sponsor house. Sheesh. That hadn't occurred to her until she saw several bikini pieces among the litter.

The downstairs was unoccupied so she headed upstairs calling again, "Raj?" No response and it made her edgy.

She opened each door as she reached it. Bathroom. Bong on the sink. Great. Toilet seat up and the floor moist-looking. Ick.

Bedroom, big mess, but nothing. Linen closet. Bedroom/study. All the rooms festooned with Hawai'ian, or faux Hawai'ian, stuff. Kapa lampshades, petroglyph themed linens, more canoe paddles, a heavy lava poi pounder in the study used as a paper weight. Last bedroom before the upstairs lanai that faced the ocean. The door was already open but she pushed it fully before stepping inside. "Raj?" He sat unmoving on a messy bed. "Raj? You okay? Find your board?"

He turned wet eyes to her. "Yeah. I did."

She glanced around the room as she came toward the bed. No people, but she saw his board—broken, with graffiti scribbled across it.

"What happened?"

"I don't know. This happened."

"Anyone here when you came?"

"No. Only this. Who would do this?"

"I don't know sweetie. I don't see any other boards. Where are they?"

"Everybody's at the beach so with them. Extras on the lanai down stairs. Mine wasn't there so I looked around. Found it. My lucky board."

Raj's board was special. His dad had it made for him, proportioned just right, with 'Raj' emblazoned across a stylized wave. Raj also had boards from Bad Boyz Beach, which he had to ride in competition, but this was his 'lucky' board. He rode it in warm ups, practices, for fun. It went on all his surf trips and he truly believed it brought him luck. Maybe it did.

"I'm so sorry. Maybe we can find out who did it."

"That stupid house chaperone was supposed to take care of it. You can't just break a board. It's super hard. I mean in waves, you can, but someone would have to work really hard to do it. This is on purpose, fo' real. And it's not like they couldn't tell whose board. Even if you nevah meet me, you know it's my board. Everyone gotta lucky something." He trailed away, trying hard not to cry.

"Sure looks like someone thinks you're a threat on the waves, bud. I guess that's good news."

"Yeah. Great news. My dad gonna kill me."

"No, of course he won't. This wasn't your fault. Maybe we don't tell him for a while, yeah?"

"Yeah." Raj picked up the two pieces. "Let's go. I gotta practice." He led the way downstairs to the lanai fronting the beach. A low dry stone wall surrounded the small yard. Another wrought iron gate gave beach access, but it was a token of closure, since the wall was low enough to step over. Better to watch the surf. The tight salt-resistant grass was covered in more surf detritus, empty beer bottles, a barbecue and orphaned rubber slippers. A rack under the overhang made by the second story lanai housed the boards.

Raj silently handed his broken board to K.O. as he selected one from the rack. She was happy to see it was bright orange with a black stripe and BBB in graffiti-style writing swirled over all. She'd be able to see that board from the beach.

"'Kay Auntie. I go." He was so deflated and dejected K.O. debated whether to talk him out of practicing. Maybe his focus wouldn't be on the water. She was about to mention it when he said, "Try wait." He leaned the board against the rack and disappeared into the house. A moment later he returned with a piece of paper. "Here. Now you don't have to move the car. You can stay with me?" It was mostly a question. He handed her a BBB residential parking pass.

"Thanks. This is great. Where did you get this?"

"Jet has them for the guys old enough to drive. Not everyone brought a car so we share."

"Of course I'll stay. You wanna get set up and I'll put your board in the car where it'll be safe, okay?"

"T'anks, eh?" He shuffled out the gate onto the sand.

K.O. watched him go and her heart contracted for him, his shoulders bent, his step hesitant. A teenaged girl ran over to Raj and magically, his shoulders straightened and his step lifted.

"Ah, the miracle of teenage hormones." K.O. smiled and grabbed Raj's broken board and the parking pass. She put the pieces in the trunk and a little pang of nostalgia hit as she remembered the last time it went in the trunk it didn't fit. She'd had to bungee it closed with the tail sticking out.

She grabbed her emergency beach kit, which she'd taken to carrying in the car at all times since she became in charge of Raj. Normally her fair skin didn't lend itself to a lot of beach time, but now she found herself unexpectedly at the beach. Often. So her 'kit' had super strength sunscreen, a beach hat she called a satellite dish, a towel, a water bottle and granola bars. She also found a folded straw beach mat at the bottom of her trunk and a water-stained paperback which she also threw in the bag.

She tossed the parking pass on the dash and then went two houses down to the public access path, not wanting to cut through the dark house again. The 'scene of the crime.'

The beach was packed and she couldn't see Raj, but she set up camp on a rise, back from the water in the shade of a scraggly palm. Not a lot of protection since it was a bit after noon, but she would move along with the sun to stay in the shade until Raj's heat.

*   *   *   *

Raj shuffled the sand as he walked. Not only was he bummed, but it was hot. He tried to stir

101

it with his feet. The practice board weighed a ton compared to his own board, and he wondered if he should have taken a bit more time to choose. He'd been so thrown at the destruction of his lucky board, the gift from his father. This board was also longer than his. He would not make a good showing if the board wasn't right. He was about to go back to the house and try again, but Kahana ran up to him.

"They called your name. You gotta go. Why you so late?" she said all in one breath.

He straightened up and tried to jog but the board was too heavy. He was able to speed up a little and made it to check in on time.

"What happened to you?" Jet was right in his face, eyes bulging, sweat dripping. "You almost missed your shot. I better not have made a mistake with you."

"No, I just had to get a board. Sorry." Raj had never seen him like this.

"Hurry up. You're white today. Get moving. Your heat's the next. Do not screw this up." Jet thrust a white jersey at him. "Get ready, wait over there." He almost pushed him down the beach.

Raj stopped about half way after Jet had gone back to the judging stand. He stuck his huge orange board upright and pulled on the white jersey. Kahana ran up to him.

"What's wrong?"

"Jet's mad at me. I never see him like this. And someone broke my lucky board so now I got this piece of crap." Raj felt his eyes burn. Not in front of a girl.

"Oh, man. I know! Leave that thing. You don't have much time." She raced up the slight crest to another group of surfers. He followed more slowly.

"Hey, Dylan," she hollered. "Dylan, this Raj. Raj, my brother. You guys about the same size, can use your board or what?"

Both Dylan and Raj mirrored surprise. "Uh," Dylan said.

"No, it's okay," Raj said.

"Really?" Kahana thrust out her chin. "You guys, this is important. Raj has to qualify. They gave him a stupid board and it's not like you're going to need it right now, brah." She poked her brother in the ribs.

"Sure," Dylan said. "If I can't be in it, my board might as well be. It's a BBB so it works, right?"

"Wow, that's really, uh, I don't know. Thanks, brah."

"Ahh, your heat's going down!" She grabbed Raj and dragged him to his group. Dylan's board felt like his old board. If he closed his eyes, it might be. He let that thought settle over him and then he dismissed it. He focused on the job. He dropped to his knees and borrowed some wax. He was a little behind the others, but Dylan took good care of this board, so he felt ready.

His heat was called and the group paddled out. He'd had no time to watch the sets so he did the best he could now. The sky was pale blue-gray and the waves smooth and huge. Larger than the day of his super ride. Those waves had been rough however, so the ride scarier in his mind. These rose like sky scrapers but were even, like a machine cranked them out all the same. He had no time to ponder it because the horn sounded and he needed a wave. Not any ride would do, but he needed the highest score. He wanted to beat Aliki. The senior man had done nothing but give attitude so he was going to give some back.

Sitting outside the waves on the rising swell gave him a bird's eye view of the beach; he could only imagine what it would look like on a wave. The lull between waves brought the sound of jet skis to him. It reassured him that the rescue team was ready. No lifeguard alone would be able to help anyone in this monster surf, so jet skis towing rescue boards like little trailers patrolled alongside the sets, ready to dart in and nab a stranded surfer. He'd seen it a lot but had never experienced it. *Not because he was so great*, he mused, *but because he'd not been in waves like this very much.*

The wave built behind him. He felt the water gather, pulling him back as he flattened himself to paddle. It rose like a cartoon, foamy hat stretching up, small curls like arms reaching for him. The sweet moment where the wave and he met with the same goal, to get to the beach, was always a rush. He knew he had caught it and his feet moved of their own accord, feeling the board, sensing the pulse of the wave beneath, threatening to capsize his little stick and plunge him five stories into water hard as concrete.   The water was a solid rollercoaster, and he rode with utter joy, up and down the wave like his board was his private coaster car. He moved forward on his board and the back rose along with the rising wave, but he stuck it. He didn't dare look to the crowd on the sand, but he was sure he had their attention and support.

The green room closed around him, the tunnel of water stretching forward with a pin prick of foam flecked sky growing larger as he rode toward it. A shadow passed him in the wall and he though *dolphin*. Good omen. They loved to play in the waves and many a cold day was made less lonesome by the companionship of dolphins.

He shot out of the tunnel and a flash of orange barely missed him. He ducked and nearly lost his balance. His wave was petering out and he went over the backside to recover. The wave continued on, less wild, smaller, tamer. In the swirl he saw the bright orange BBB board he was supposed to ride.

A flurry of activity as the jet skis roared around him, trying to find the surfer that belonged to the board, he assumed.

I wonder who took my board? That's weird. All the contestants have a board here and no amateurs would be dumb enough to be out in this. Would they? Would they get kicked out? Could you 'reserve' the waves for the contest? He just didn't know enough. No time to think because the half-way horn sounded and he only had a little time to catch another wave.

The next set was rougher and not quite as big. He caught one, but knew it was unremarkable. Although he did his best, he didn't get the same feeling of power and ownership of his other wave.

The horn sounded again and he paddled in. His group was done for the day. He hoped his one ride, which felt amazing, looked that way to the judges. He hadn't seen any other heats so he had no idea of the scores. *Maybe a lot of guys had amazing rides today*, he thought glumly.

He trudged up the beach and Kahana ran to greet him, bubbling over with support. He was glad for the company but now he worried about his score and what happened to the rider of the orange board.

"Hey, t'anks again for the board," he said to Dylan when he reached the group right where he left them.

"That was so awesome!" Dylan clasped his hand. "So glad my board got a ride li' dat! Maybe it'll remember da next time I'm out there."

"Yeah, I think was more your board den me, brah," Raj joked. "I bettah check my scores, you nevah know." He could tell the group, particularly Kahana, wanted him to stay and talk story, but he didn't feel like it. He was worn out and more tired than usual. The high from the great ride had quickly mellowed and he actually wanted to find his Auntie. She was a good person to bounce ideas off of and maybe she would know why he felt so down. He looked around for her but didn't see her. It was pretty crowded. He had to find out his standing for the day. He almost didn't want to. All the waves were pretty great so maybe a lot of guys got awesome rides. He passed a large group buzzing with energy. He saw a rescue Jet Ski pulled up on the beach and a life guard in the group. No one was hurt but he zig zagged over to eaves drop.

He didn't get a chance to ask anything because the group parted and he saw his orange board. With a big bite mark. He stood unmoving and took in the conversation. Apparently, the shadow was not a dolphin, but a thirteen foot Tiger shark, and at some point had taken a chunk out of the board. With or without a rider. Raj was supposed to be on that board, but the last time he'd seen it was when he'd left it on the beach and gone with Kahana. *I guess no one knew I wasn't on it unless they watched me, not the board. It's not like you can train a shark to attack a board, right? Now I'm being stupid. Definitely shook up because someone broke my board and maybe tried to make me miss my qualifying heat. Or mess up my head so I can't surf. But it would be a stretch to think a shark attacked my board because of me. Right?*

The judges knew where he was by his white jersey and number, not the board. But someone else might not know. Someone who watched him leave the sponsor house with that giant, neon, orange target. He definitely needed to find his Auntie. What if she saw the damaged board and thought something had happened to him? She would look by the stand after the heat. That's where they always met.

He slipped and slid as quickly as he could back up the beach dodging spectators and surfers to the judges' stand. They had just finished scoring. That couldn't be right. He'd tied with Buddy Soarez? Aliki, Myles Freeh and Eldon Hayashi hadn't surfed yet, but of the previous competitors, he was in second. Granted, the other two top guys hadn't gone yet, but it felt good. A bubble of pure pleasure eclipsed his funk. He was above Tai Phillips from Billabong and Terry Sutton from BBB—both excellent. Amazing.

Suddenly he was starving. He wanted food, he wanted his Auntie, he wanted to stay and soak up all the energy and excitement. He wanted to call his folks. That brought him down a notch. Reminded him about his board and that he'd have to tell his dad at some point. Maybe not today. No Auntie but he had to eat. He'd check the sponsor house and get something there. After all, he was a member of the team. The smells of barbecue were killing him as the food trucks cranked out plate lunches and all the houses along the beach held back to back parties.

Chapter 8

K.O. had to use the bathroom. She should have gone when they were in the team sponsor house. Rats. She was miles from *da luas*, as the portapotties were known, and the sponsor house, icky as it had been, was only a couple minutes' walk. She would go back.

She didn't know what color jersey Raj would end up with, but she could sure spot that orange board. She hoped she didn't miss his ride, but not having a choice, she hustled up to the back gate. All the neighboring houses were alive with action, but the BBB team house was quiet. She didn't know if that was 'normal.' She knew nothing about this sport and since the whole team was competing, it made sense everyone was gone. *I guess.*

The back door was open the way they'd left it. She by-passed the downstairs bathroom in favor of one of the upstairs facilities. Maybe the master? If fewer people used it, maybe it wouldn't be as gross. Or she could do a quick clean first. She didn't have a lot of time. *At least if I explode, no one will notice.*

The master bedroom door was ajar. She shoved it open and raced to the bathroom, grateful it was reasonably clean. She washed her hands and came out. *So much better.*

She glanced at the edge of the bed where Raj had sat not too long ago. Poor kid. So sad. *I hope he's doing better.* She crossed to the sliders and opened them to the lanai. The view from here was amazing. Unlike the front garden, the back was very sparse, again, to keep the optimal view. Two palms flanked the yard and nothing else was above the height of the squatty boundary wall. Some surfer-proof grass and naupaka bushes for contrast. She squinted and shaded her eyes with her hand. The sun was low enough to make glittering streaks bounce across the water into her brain. She only saw blobs in the water. She should have brought her binocs, but she'd left them in her 'beach kit' to mark her territory under the ratty palm on the shore.

"Shoots. Better get back to the beach. Don't want to miss my boy after all this." She came back to the doorway, black spots dancing before her eyes from sun glare. She closed them to let them adjust. A moment passed and the spots receded behind closed lids. She opened them and stepped inside, immediately stopping again.

"That is *not* what I think it is." A glimpse of a bare foot under the messy drape of bedspread. Invisible to anyone entering the room or sitting on the bed, for that matter, as Raj had done. She dropped to her knees, praying it was someone hiding, but she didn't think so. *If I'd been under the bed, I'd be curled into the smallest ball ever*, she thought.

"Hey, you okay?" She touched the foot. Cold. Ick. She scooched around the base of the bed trying to get a better look. On the far side, nearest the hall door, she saw his face. Asian or white, male and young. One of the other surfers from the team? She couldn't tell for sure with the damage. Bloody, matted hair, glazed eyes and mouth slightly open. She didn't touch anything else after she fruitlessly felt for a carotid pulse. No matter how many bodies she'd seen on the job, she never quite got used to it. She struggled to return to some semblance of professional distance. She returned downstairs to find a phone. She tried to remember what she touched, and what it looked like when she and Raj had been here. What, an hour ago? She glanced at her watch. Only an hour. But the body could have been there already when she and Raj looked for his board. *His* board. She hadn't noticed any blood or hair. It could have been used as a weapon. The fin—skeg—Raj kept reminding her, was a pretty decent sharp edged tool. Lots of surfers got hurt by it in the waves. If the board was already broken that would make a more convenient weapon. On the counter dividing the kitchen from the living room, she found a phone. She reported a body but had no idea of the address. She hoped the District Two guys could figure it out by "look for the turtle gate." Geez, she should know better. When they'd been looking for the house earlier, she'd forgotten the house number the second she realized she

111

couldn't see any addresses at all on most of the buildings. Even street signs were hard to find with the trees and bushes bordering the roads. *Great detective work, Ogden.* She did remember her patrol Crown Vic was parked in front, and gave them the plate number.

Somberly, she reminded herself to move it once the first official car rolled up. Dispatch didn't seem upset that she had no idea where she was. *I guess it's common up here*, she thought. *Or maybe the dispatcher was nice because I'm HPD, too.*

She trudged out the front door, wide open, too. *Did I close it when I put Raj's board in my trunk?* She thought she did since she wasn't coming back through the house, but she truly didn't remember. She stayed on the slate path, now mindful of foot and finger prints. That house was a mess. Investigators would be there for hours taking prints and bagging junk for evidence. Having watched a lot of crime scene work, she knew they'd take everything that could possibly be related. "You never know what will turn out to be important," a little blonde haole Scientific Investigation Section investigator told her once. "I'd rather take my time here and now, and take it all, than realize later I might have missed something."

K.O. suddenly hoped that investigator and her partner got this case. She moved her car as far as she could, which wasn't far. The road dead-ended in some Ironwood trees four houses down. She put her light bar on the roof to make it official. She reminded herself to give them Raj's board for

112

evidence. Raj! She hoped he was having fun. She couldn't leave the crime scene and there was nothing she could do about it. But hope. *Been doing a lot of that,* she mused.

For now, she went back to the turtle gate to wait and flag down the cops. It wasn't long before the local patrol car showed up. One by one, official vehicles arrived, filling the little street with swirling lights and blue uniforms. She was relegated to the back burner, but on standby to tell her same story a thousand times. She knew the drill.

*　　*　　*　　*

Raj sped through the beachfront gate to the sponsor house at top speed. He was starving now. He screeched to a halt as he took in about a million cops. His stomach dropped and he almost turned and ran back out. Gut response.

"Hey," a burly guy in a suit called out. "Kid. Come 'ere."

Raj was pretty respectful of authority, but this was way out of normal and scared the crap out of him. He froze.

The cop, as evidenced by the badge on his belt, was already moving to him anyway. "Whatchu doing here?"

"I, uh, looking for my Auntie. What happened? Is she okay?"

"Dis your Auntie house?"

"No. It's . . . I'm a surfer . . ." words dried up.

"Everybody a surfer here, brah. It's okay, kid. I'm Detective Keahi. What's your name?"

"Raj. Um, Dela Cruz. I mean Ben." Raj didn't feel so good.

"Hey, sit down 'Raj, I mean Ben.' Take it easy." Keahi guided him to a hardwood dining room chair and plopped him in it. "Tell me why you here."

Raj saw people with big brief case boxes moving around, taking prints and tweezing things. The majority of the foot traffic went up and down the stairs to the second floor.

"What's going on? What happened? I'm looking for my Auntie. Did something happen to her?"

"Who your Auntie? Why would she be here if it's not her house? Do you know da owner?"

"No. Dis a rental." Raj gulped air, hoping to keep from throwing up. *What if something had happened to his Auntie? What would happen to him?*

"Yeah? So, how come you heah?"

"This house rented by the Bad Boyz Beach surf team. I'm on the team. I no stay heah, I stay wit' my Auntie, but da sponsor, Jet, he say we can all use da house, you know?"

Keahi nodded and signaled to another cop to give him the water bottle he held. "Here, take a drink. Try stay calm."

Raj gratefully drank and felt a little better. "Where my Auntie? Something happen to her?" His stomach flopped again.

114

"Who your Auntie and why would she be here? You say it's da surf house, yeah? She surf?"

"No, but she watch out for me. I thought maybe she came here when I couldn't find her on the beach after my ride."

Suddenly his day caught up with him. His anxiety, the destruction of his precious board, his terrifying, gratifying ride, the shark, the orange board with the bite out of it, was all too much. Before Keahi could stop him, Raj bolted out the back sliders to the yard and threw up. For a large man, Keahi moved quickly and was holding him. Raj felt partially restrained and partially reassured. *Probably both* flitted through his brain.

"Raj!" his Auntie's voice called. Next she felt her arms around him and he let the tears flow.

"Are you okay?" they asked each other. He nodded and her answer was to hug him tighter.

"Detective Keahi?" K.O. asked. "What's he doing here? This is my nephew. He's on the surf team. I didn't know he'd come back to the house."

"K.O. Congrats on your promotion. It's okay. He didn't get upstairs."

K.O. nodded her thanks. "We were both up there earlier, so our prints and maybe hair will be there. Neither of us saw anything then. Did you tell him yet?"

"No. I didn't know who he was or why he was here." Keahi turned to Raj. "Feeling better?"

Raj nodded. "What happened? Why isn't anyone telling me?"

"Let's sit," K.O. said, nodding to the chairs on the patio. Keahi joined them.

"Raj." K.O. exhaled a steadying breath. "Something happened upstairs. We don't know when it happened yet. Could have been before or after we were there, but I found a body under the bed."

"The bed I was sitting on?" Raj's eyes got huge.

K.O. nodded. "I don't know how to tell you this, but he was murdered." She put her hand on his and squeezed. "I don't know who it is. I mean, I couldn't tell, but it's not Jet or Aliki, I know that."

"Jeez." Raj's tanned skin, already pale from the initial shock, got another shade lighter. His lips stood out like he wore lipstick.

"Just breathe, brah," Keahi said. "I need to take your prints, okay?"

Raj looked to K.O. "It's okay," she said. "For elimination." Raj raised his eyebrows in question. "We were both in the house, so when they find our prints, they'll know it wasn't us."

Raj nodded. Keahi rose and got a print kit. "We already got hers on file. We worked together before, so we know her crimes," he joked, pointing at K.O.

Raj gave him a watery smile.

After the prints, Keahi skillfully questioned him on his movements, patiently listening to the surf parts which had nothing to do with the crime scene. "Congratulations, Raj. My son surfs up here, too, but not pro. He's a good guy. Maybe I should get you two together sometime."

116

"I don't live here, sir. I stay with my Auntie for contests. But it would be nice to meet your son."

"Might be good for him." Keahi stood and turned to K.O. "I need to ask you about the sponsor and go over again what you saw."

A commotion by the front door drew their attention. Keahi went to find out what was happening. K.O. and Raj exchanged a glance and followed. She mouthed, *don't touch anything*, and he rolled his eyes, *I know*.

A young man stood in the foyer arguing with the cop with a clipboard in charge of logging all entrances and exits to the crime scene.

"But I live here. What's happening?" the young man said.

Detective Keahi reached him, trailed by K.O. and Raj. "Who are you?"

"That's Robert. The house chaperone!" Raj blurted.

"Yeah, I'm the chaperone for the house. Robert Goto. What's going on?"

"You have some I.D.?" Keahi asked.

"In my room. I was at the beach. I don't take my wallet to the beach."

"You didn't do such a great job today," Keahi said. "Let's get your I.D. and talk." He led him upstairs.

Raj was relieved that his auntie stayed with him. "Okay. Raj, you gotta go back to the beach or you done for today?" she asked.

"I'm done. I got my scores, but I can go and watch for a while if you gonna be here."

"Sounds good. Can you watch my stuff by the palm tree? I'll meet you there in an hour and we'll go, okay?" She obviously didn't want him coming back to the house again.

Raj went out the beach gate and then looked back. His Auntie stood watching him. He hoped he wasn't in trouble. He hoped *she* wasn't in trouble. He looked for a palm tree anchored by his Auntie's bag, recognizable by the big turtle stitched onto the straw.

*   *   *   *

K.O. watched Raj exit the gate for a moment, relieved he was okay with her going into 'work mode.' K.O. vaguely remembered seeing Goto at the meeting in Jet's hotel room, but since he didn't talk, she had erased him.

Up close, Goto looked to be in his mid-to late 30s. Has-been surfer, maybe? Hired to babysit because he couldn't surf anymore? K.O. speculated. Round spectacles, fly away dark hair, and smooth pale skin except for crow's feet around the eyes. That skin did not spend all day every day at the beach, for sure. If he was a surfer, back in the day, it had been a while. She further assessed his slim body. He looked wiry, but not surfing fit. K.O. waited for Keahi. Eventually he and Goto returned to the living room.

"When can we use the house again?" Goto asked.

"When we're done. And I don't know when that will be. It's a crime scene, and until the investigators clear it, it remains closed."

"What am I supposed to do with the guys staying here?"

"I have no idea."

"Can we get our stuff? What do I tell them?"

Keahi sighed. "Tomorrow I'll ask if you and your people can pack a few things *under supervision*. It depends, so don't count on it. Give me a list of everyone staying here and everyone with access to the house. Keys?"

Goto shook his head. "Only me and the team owner have keys, but we nevah lock it." He scribbled a list of names onto the notepad Keahi handed him. "Shit. Well, can I use the phone? I have to call the owner and let him know."

"The owner of the house? Who is that?"

Goto looked like Keahi was crazy. "No. The owner of the team. The owner of the company sponsoring *the team*! He has no idea what's going on."

Unless Jet did it, K.O. thought. *Then he's completely up to speed.*

Keahi nodded and Goto picked up the same phone she'd used to call the police earlier. Conveniently located on the divider between kitchen and where she sat at the dining table.

Goto covered the mouthpiece but she heard bits of conversation. Jet was not happy and Goto made placating noises. Some discussion of paying for the house out of a fund, and no way there was another house to rent for fifty miles. She gathered Jet would have to give up his 'meeting room' at the hotel to put up the surfers for at least a couple days.

119

That didn't seem too bad to K.O. or warrant the yelling she heard from Jet's end of the phone. Goto hung up a little shaken.

"Oh, Mr. Goto. One more thing. Follow me please." Keahi led him out the front and K.O. obligingly followed too.

The body bag rested on a gurney outside the medical examiner's van doors, ready for loading and transport.

"Maybe you can save us some time," Keahi said and unzipped the bag. "Do you know this man?"

K.O. knew why he was doing it so cavalierly: to get a reaction, to catch Goto off-guard as well as get an I.D. They couldn't run the body's prints until they got back to the lab.

Goto's face went even whiter. "That's Eldon Hayashi. He's on the team. He's the best on the BBB team. Oh, God. What a loss." He swayed and K.O. stepped forward and set a steadying hand on his arm. If he passed out he'd smash his face in, much like Hayashi's was. Hmm, now that she had a name, she remembered the victim resembled a surfer at the meeting. The face was so damaged on one side that it pulled all the features out of proportion. She was glad the ruined side had been mostly down on the carpet. She was doubly glad she'd been the one to find him, and not Raj.

Keahi continued to question Goto, but K.O. had a question of her own. She backtracked and went upstairs. Apparently once she was 'logged in,' she was allowed free rein. That uni would probably get in trouble for it later, but she wasn't going to point it out. She was careful not to touch any walls, the bannister, doorknobs, etc. and she stopped in the doorway of the master bedroom. As she'd hoped, Jeanine, the little blonde haole investigator and her partner, Ken, were on it.

"Aloha, Jeanine. Howzit?"

"K.O.! What you doing here? Not your beat, eh?"

"No, just got lucky and found da body. I with my nephew, he's surfing da contests up here."

"Oh, man. I'm sorry."

"I have a question. Unofficially."

"Sure. If it's evidence-stuff, I cannot."

"I know. About time of death. You have yet?"

"Not officially."

"That's okay. I only want a guess."

"Some time around noon, maybe couple hours before? He just starting rigor when we get here. Hardly froze at all yet."

"So, what's that mean?"

"Three hours, mebbe. But not official, you know? M.E. give you that. Why?"

"Cuz, when I find him that means he got it not too long before. Creepy. Maybe da killah still around then." K.O.'s heart constricted thinking of Raj alone in the house for even a few minutes with a murderer nearby and a body under the bed.

"Oh, yeah, das bad. I'm sorry. I gotta get back to it." She waved her arms to indicate all the cataloging they had to do.

"Yeah, I let you go. Thanks. See you."

K.O. went downstairs to wait for Keahi. He joined her shortly to review her earlier story. Keahi took her through her first and second entries into the house. She mentioned the team meeting where she thought she had seen Hayashi at ten, but didn't know when he left. After that, she and Raj had stayed to talk to Jet. Did that alibi him? Maybe. Timing-wise, her only conclusion was that she could not be sure the body wasn't already under the bed when she and Raj had been in the room.

"How much time did Raj have alone in the bedroom before you came in?"

"A minute or two." *He can't seriously think Raj killed that guy? Or even shoved him under the bed?* She knew Keahi was being thorough, but really. That also meant that Raj would have had time, following her logic as it applied to Jet. So could anyone from the team or the beach. She sighed.

Someone had done a number on that skull. Rage and probably something personal at stake. She didn't think it was an interrupted burglary. Who could tell, the house was so messy? But the things of the greatest value she'd seen were the surfboards, and the surfers, and they were at the beach. Except for the back-up boards. But even a board worth a couple thousand, was that worth killing over? She'd seen drug-related crimes over less money, but this didn't feel right. The bathroom bong notwithstanding. Resigned, she acknowledged to herself that she had no idea if there were drugs or lots of cash or jewelry available. Prior to this morning, she didn't even know the sponsor house existed. Raj did, however. She blew out a breath. *Maybe he did know something he didn't want to tell even her.* A sobering thought.

The house was a typical rental, albeit an upscale one. Furniture looked okay, but not high end. Be silly to rent to surfers on a beach front with best quality stuff. The art was standard, inexpensive 'local' flavor, the kind she saw working special duty at the Aloha Swap Meet. No piles of money or mountains of coke graced the koa end tables when she and Raj had come to look for his board. Maybe there was a hidden safe. No way she'd find out about that. At least not yet.

Granted she hadn't searched the drawers and closets like HPD was doing, but she'd bet they wouldn't come up with anything of value.

Keahi stopped his note-taking. "Okay, this sponsor. You know him, yeah? Your nephew being on the team. Name?"

"Jet. I can't remember his last name. That Goto guy will know. It's not that famous a company and they're trying to move up in the surf world. Raj surfed the first two contests in the Triple Crown, but I wasn't there much at all for those. I didn't meet Jet or anyone until this contest. This is the biggest showing of their surfers and surf gear, I understand. Also, the first time they've sponsored surfers. Raj told me they were here in the past but only to sell surf wear, give out stuff to surfers, try to generate interest. In the last couple years they've really pushed to make a name for themselves. They're not Vans or Billabong, but who knows, in ten years, maybe."

Keahi was writing as fast as he could. "Okay, you mentioned another name before with Jet. Aliki. Who's that?"

"He's on the team, too. Old and sort of fading surfer. Used to be tops, but is now an alternate for BBB. Always seems mad, and I usually see him with Jet. Like his assistant or something."

"When you say old, how old."

"34."

"If 34 is old, I'm dead," Keahi mumbled.

K.O. laughed. "I know what you mean, but in the surf world, that's pretty old. Raj is fifteen and he's the baby of the sport this year. He's only got a few good years to make it. This is his first year. He's an alternate, like Aliki, and that seems to really piss Aliki off."

"Okay, I'd bettah find dis Jet and Aliki. You keep tabs on Raj. We don't know who did it or any motive yet. If dat person saw you guys at da house, you nevah know. Mebbe he t'ink you guys saw something. Anyway, stay alert. I'll be in touch."

K.O. went out the front, racking her brain to remember any small detail that might help. Nothing new popped up. She should have paid more attention at the meeting. She negotiated her Crown Vic around the fleet of official vehicles. No scrapes against the property walls, but a hibiscus bush would never be the same. She didn't want Raj to have to come by the house again. She parked illegally on the ironwood needle strewn beach fronting the jammed parking lot. She left her blue lights on, not completely kosher, but she wouldn't be long. She jogged past all the booths and food trucks to the soft sand and made it back to her palm.

Raj sat, arms folded over raised knees, looking toward the waves, but K.O. knew he wasn't watching the surf. His drawn features and tense body told her he was going over the day again and again, just like she was.

Chapter 9

K.O. stepped in front of Raj so she didn't startle him. His glazed expression slowly refocused on her. "Ready to go?" she asked.

"Yeah." He stood like an old man. "Who was it? Do they know?"

"Eldon Hayashi." She grabbed her beach bag. She tried to switch gears. "It's been a rough day. On the bright side, you qualified, right?"

"Yeah. But, when I checked my scores, not everyone had surfed yet. Eldon hadn't gone and now I know why." He sounded a little weepy.

"Hey, it's okay. I know it's upsetting. Do you want to check the score board before we go? See if anything's changed? Does that affect your shot tomorrow?"

As if in answer, the sky darkened and a chill wind blew up, rattling the sponsor banners on the judges' stand.

"I guess I should."

"Sweetie, I know this is a terrible thing, but listen to me." K.O. stopped and turned him to face her. "You had nothing to do with this; there was

126

nothing either of us could do. This is your big chance, so you take it. Do you think these top guys stopped when something got thrown in their way? No, they didn't. They figured out a way around it and kept going. You concentrate on your job and I'll do mine. I'll make sure you're where you need to be and that you're fed. Theresa is in charge of puncturing your legs. Think of it as cat acupuncture. Catupuncture."

That got a small smile out of Raj. "Okay."

They continued to the stand and read the boards. Nothing was mentioned about Eldon, his name still listed. Aliki, however, had missed his heat. Odd.

"Auntie? What does that mean?" K.O. knew Raj didn't mean in surfing terms. He meant in terms of Eldon's body under the bed, which is what K.O. was thinking, too.

"I don't know. You see him anyplace?" They both scanned the beach. "Hey," K.O. said to a guy in a yellow tee with credentials hanging from an official Pipeline lanyard, "You seen Aliki Gomes lately?"

"Nah," the man said, not even looking at her, continuing down the beach.

"Well, that was helpful. Let's go. I'm done with this place for today."

"Wait. I gotta see the schedule fo' tomorrow."

"I'll be at the food trucks." K.O. had had enough. She wanted to be at home, where things were normal. She did not understand this sport, and did not understand the way the pro circuit worked, much less the territorial sniping, and now a murder, that went along with it.

Raj was back in a few minutes. "I dropped down a little, but I'm higher than Aliki, so if I keep on going, my scores might put me in the running!"

His spirits have lifted, thought K.O. "Great news. Let's get you home and fed and think about what movie you want to watch tonight. We can stop at the video store on the way back."

She wondered if she should talk to Jet about Raj's chances or his 'career' as Jet was so fond of putting it. She decided to pass, knowing his hands would be full with Detective Keahi and all of HPD on him. That thought made her smile.

She wondered about Jet as a suspect. She couldn't fathom a situation where he'd have a motive to kill his best surfer and lessen his chances to play with the big boys like Vans and Billabong. She'd learned these winnings were big money and the sponsor obviously reaped the benefits of that. Jet had opportunity, since no one to paid attention to where he was, and being the sponsor, he had no set schedule like the surfers did. *All the surfers had opportunity*, K.O. mused. *They all would have left the meeting, come to the BBB house and gotten their boards. Timing was interesting, since it was a small window to get Eldon alone. For that matter, anyone could come from the beach side and no one would know or care, because everyone is right on the shore. Hide in plain sight.* K.O. was glad it was Keahi's job.

They reached the Crown Vic in silence, K.O. doing her 'suspect' thing and Raj probably accepting his gold medal or something, whatever they got for winning this contest. A new pair of Vans shoes? Wait. Something about shoes eluded her. *Oh, well. It'll come back. It usually does.* She smiled to herself and pulled onto the highway.

"What you like for dinner? You know yet?" K.O. remembered he'd thrown up earlier so he was running on empty.

"Not sure. Thinking homemade plate lunch?"

"Man, you can live on those things!" Since it was his favorite meal, K.O. and Raj had learned to concoct a homemade plate lunch of chicken katsu, rice and macaroni salad. K.O. used low-fat mayo as a concession to all the starch, and Raj invented an amazing katsu sauce with ketchup and spices. K.O. was in favor of anything that began with ketchup.

"Done. What about the movie? Any ideas?"

"How about *Basic Instinct?*"

Even though she was into a curvy part of the trip, she risked a sideways glance and saw his smile starting.

"Nice try, bud." He laughed outright. "Let's see if they have *Batman* or *A Few Good Men.*"

"Seen it, and that sounds boring."

"Fine. What about *Alien 3?*"

"Okay."

"You have to hold my hand. I about had a cow during the first *Alien.*"

"I'll put Teresa in the middle and we can both hold her hands."

At home, K.O. breaded chicken breasts and tofu, Raj made the katsu sauce and started the rice cooker. K.O. boiled macaroni and put it in the freezer to cool faster.

As they ate, K.O. remembered she was supposed to tell Keahi about Aliki missing his heat. The evening had gone so pleasantly, despite the day, she was reluctant to break it up.

"Hey, before we start the movie I'm going to shower. Can you put away the leftovers please?"

He rose to comply and she used her bedroom phone to call Keahi. He didn't pick up of course, but she left a succinct message. "Hey John, it's K.O. I'm sure you'll find this out but it might save you some time. Aliki Gomes on the BBB surf team missed his qualifying heat this afternoon. It was around the time Raj and I were in the sponsor house. I didn't see him at all on the beach today, which isn't that surprising, but he's a pain and usually finds a way to be in Raj's face. Call me if you have questions. I have court tomorrow, but I'm dropping Raj off at the beach for more heats."

She hung up and thought about what she'd said. She'd have to leave Raj alone at the beach because she could not miss this court date. She came out of the bedroom as Raj was turning on the loaded dishwasher.

"Wow, thanks. I didn't mean for you to do all the clean-up."

"No worries. Easy only two of us."

"We need to talk about tomorrow, okay? Sit down." They sat at the dining table. "I have to go to court tomorrow. I can't postpone and I can't miss it."

"I know. You said."

"I am not comfortable leaving you at the beach all day after what happened."

"I won't go into the team house."

"Well, you can't, it's a crime scene. But that's not what I mean. Whoever killed Eldon might have seen us there. They might think we saw something. Even if that's not the case, I just don't like leaving you without any support given the risky nature of the contest now."

"Well, Jet didn't do it. He's supposed to take care of me, anyway. He knows that."

Ah, spoken like a true young person. He was so naive it would be cute if it weren't dangerous.

"I didn't see Jet after the meeting today. Some promoter he is." K.O. tried unsuccessfully to hide her skepticism.

"What about the chaperone? He's in charge of the house anyway, and I guess the guys staying there. He can watch me."

Oh, boy. More people she knew nothing about. It was true, it was Goto's job to chaperone, but he hadn't done such a great job of it. K.O.'s brain whirled furiously. She had to make this work. If she forced Raj to give up his big chance, he might never get over it.

"Auntie, you said yourself not to let this get in the way of my career. Now you letting it. I'm not going to do anything stupid. I'm careful. I'll

stay away from the house and strangers, I promise.
I'm not ten."

"I know." She looked at him, now fifteen.
Fifteen and a *half* he would say, and she saw the
baby, the toddler, the child and the young teen all
overlaid by this gangly, loving young man
struggling for independence amid a desire to be
cared for.

He had his father's chocolate brown eyes
and dark hair, but a streak of his mother's, and
K.O.'s, stubbornness ran right down the middle.

"Okay. Here's the deal. I'm going to call
Alani and see if he can meet you there. I'll drop
you off on my way to court and you can do your
runs. But you are not to leave the beach or do
anything until Alani or I get there. Understood?"

"What if Alani can't come?" Raj asked, his
voice small.

"I'll figure something out. Even if I have to
call Keahi to get you. We'll make it work. Don't
worry. You just eat well, rest up and surf your ass
off tomorrow, okay?"

Raj's eyebrows went way up and he let out a
huge laugh at her choice of words. They both knew
she meant it. He nodded.

K.O. headed back into the bedroom to call
Alani while Raj got the video ready.

After the slightly mushy pleasantries about
how much they missed each other and when next
they would get together, K.O. filled him in on the
murder and then got down to the favor.

"Can you please meet Raj at Pipeline and
watch out for him? I don't know who to trust and I

can't get out of court tomorrow. It wasn't going to be a big deal but now with the murder, I don't feel right not having an adult there. The team sponsor is a snake oil salesman, and the chaperone let someone die on his watch. I don't know anyone else up there except the other alternate surfer who's an ass and was MIA for his qualifying heat so he's a suspect as far as I'm concerned. Like I said, I know Raj isn't a baby, but this changes everything."

Finally she wound down. After moment of silence she heard Alani's deep chuckle. She pictured his dark eyes crinkling up at the corners when he laughed, his teeth pearlescent against his skin. His Hawai'ian genes showed in his stature and gorgeous hair she loved to run her fingers through. Ahh, getting too hot in here. Focus.

"You done?" he asked.

"Yes." She was a little out of breath, but not from her monologue.

"Yes," he said.

"Yes? I am? Done?"

He laughed again. "No. Yes, I will meet Raj at the beach. I haven't seen him since last year, but I assume he looks the same?"

"Yes, but about a foot taller. We always meet at the big judges' stand. When do you think you can get there? I'll tell him to keep checking."

"Noon. I have to get an order ready to ship. It has to go out tomorrow and I have to pack it myself." Alani always packed his hand crafted koa bowls and art himself. His woodwork was renowned and he was making not only a name for himself, but a more than comfortable living from it.

133

"I have to be in court by nine so I'll drop Raj off for his heat early. He can hang out. He's a bit nervous so I'm sure he'll stay close to the judges' stand. I'll give him money so he can buy food. The way it's been going, we never know when he's surfing or what's going on until it's happening. I think his sponsor, Jet, is supposed to keep him up on it, but he's a real winner and so far hasn't been too great at it."

"I got a cell phone. I'll give you the number to give to Raj. There's a pay phone at the beach, right?"

"Yes. A cell phone? Wow."

"Yup. It weighs a ton and takes forever to charge its huge battery, but I've been trying to carry it more often for business. No one knows I have it, so I guess that's why no one's called," he joked. He gave her the number and they exchanged pleasant suggestions on how to pass the time the next chance they had to see one another.

Chapter 10

Friday dawned gray to the west; storm clouds high in the distance. K.O. made coffee and reviewed her game plan, unsure if she had covered Raj's supervision and safety to her satisfaction. She hoped the surf would remain viable since she could not get to the North Shore any sooner and none of her hand-picked Raj-sitters could change his plans if the day were cancelled. Raj was right. He was a young man, almost sixteen, and she had to trust him. Not a great feeling. She dropped kibble into Theresa's bowl and was about to rouse Raj when she heard the shower start.

She dressed in uniform for court and was already sweaty in the early humidity. Honolulu promised to be even worse. At least she'd spend the day in air conditioning. If the case went well, which she doubted, maybe she'd get back to Pipeline early. She sighed. She anticipated the case slopping over into Monday. Frustrating.

Raj was tense at breakfast too. He picked at his food.

"Anxious for today?" K.O. asked.

"Yeah. I t'ink it's getting real fo' me." He stirred his already stirred coffee.

"You're holding your breath. You do that when you're worried."

He blew out a sigh. "I know. I forgot. It's that, up to now, I been little nervous, yeah?" He glanced at her for confirmation. She nodded. "But now, I been surfing real good, and people I think way bettah den me, surfing not so good. You know?" K.O. nodded again. "So, I moving up which I nevah expect. I came heah as one alternate, and now look like I might be *in* it. So, stressin' man." He sipped his coffee.

K.O. felt for him and regretted again her decision to let him go alone. Sweat beaded his upper lip and his hairline glistened from the early humidity. K.O. switched on a seldom-used fan and adjusted it to cover them.

"So, now Eldon gets whacked and I move up again. Feels weird," he finished.

K.O. was a little shocked at his matter of fact recital of a fellow surfer's murder, but supposed that's the way he was handling it. He didn't talk 'feelings' much, so she didn't want to distract him before they parted. This could be one of the most important days of his life.

"Aliki was a no show. Does that mean you move up more?" K.O. asked.

"I guess. But only on the BBB team. I only move up in competition relative to da othah guys. Terry Sutton and Eric Lee from BBB qualified, too. I nevah see them surf yesterday, but maybe after I left. Was crazy day."

136

"Sure was. Wanna go over the game plan?"

"Not really. I get 'em." He saw her face. "But if it make you feel bettah."

"It will. You obviously can't depend on Jet right now. Don't be alone with him. If he wants to talk to you about anything, career, strategy, the lineup, fine. But only on the beach. In fact, when you're not in the water, I want you right by that judges' stand. That's where Alani's going to meet you at noon."

Raj looked about to speak and she forestalled him. "I know you don't know the schedule. Alani knows that too, and plans to spend the day there if it lasts that long. No worries. I'll give you money for food trucks and they have water and snacks by the judges' stand for competitors. Under no circumstances are you to go near that sponsor house, okay?"

"I get 'em." Raj was starting to look surly.

K.O. was worn out already. She still had to prepare for court, but figured she'd have time to review her report notes while she waited to testify. She'd been consumed with Raj but hadn't anticipated this extra worry of his safety out of the water as well. She'd slept restlessly and wished she could take the day off. No go.

"You ready?" she asked Raj.

"Yeah."

He didn't need to get anything. He wore BBB jams and a tee, rubber slippers and that was it. He had no car key, house key or wallet. K.O. made sure she had her briefcase with her reports and grabbed her purse. It felt odd to wear her uniform

and gun and then carry a purse. Oh, well. She
grabbed a small Ziploc bag and stuffed a twenty
inside.

"Here." She thrust it at him. "Put this in
your pocket for later."

"T'anks, eh." He stuffed the money into the
inner pocket of the jams. A lot of surfers tied their
car key onto the drawstring of their surf shorts, but
BBB had an inner pocket with sturdy Velcro.

K.O. tried to be cheerful on the drive north,
but her attempts fell flat so she gave up. The
weather didn't improve as they went. On the other
hand, it didn't look any worse.

She pulled into the lot at Pipeline and they
were so early it was fairly deserted. One small
consolation was that school was still in session.

"So, if you need something, go to Sunset
Beach elementary, okay?" Raj looked at her oddly.
"You know, you need help or anything."

"Like what?" He had that look like she was
overreacting. Maybe she was. *Think fast, K.O.,
don't freak him out.*

"Like da beach pay phone doesn't work.
Like that. You a kid. They let you use the phone to
call me or Alani. Oh, here. Add this to the money."
She handed him a slip of paper with Alani's cell
number on it.

"Right." But he took the paper and folded it
small, stuffing it into the plastic bag in the inner
pocket. "We good?"

"Yes. Have a great day. I'll be thinking of
you. This is the last day to qualify, yeah?"

"Uh huh."

"Kay den. You in da big time, fo' shuah. You gon' kill out deah." She laid on the pidgin and then instantly regretted her choice of words. Raj didn't seem to notice. He gave her a semblance of his old grin.

He opened the door and a wave of humidity filled the car. She watched him trot off toward the arch that welcomed everyone to the Triple Crown contest. She wondered if his name would be added to that victory list on the arch someday. She directed the A/C vent onto her face and bumped it up to MAX. The dampness in her armpits was only partially due to the weather. *Nothing could happen to that kid. Nothing.*

*   *   *   *

Raj headed toward the judges' stand. Only a few folks milled around at this hour. Auntie had to get to court through Friday rush hour traffic so he was super early. The humidity was intense and the cloud cover that had seemed so far away in Kaneohe had moved in to clamp down on the North Shore. It hovered west of the contest area, near the town of Haleiwa, but maybe it was farther away toward the mountains. Clouds and rain didn't matter as much as wind and waves.

He watched the sets roll in. So far so good. He checked the tally boards but nothing had been updated since yesterday.

"Be nice if my sponsor gave me a clue," he muttered. He settled in to wait for more people; maybe someone he knew to tell him what was going on. His own team was messed up, but he decided not to let that affect his ride. If BBB folded, he needed to catch the eye of another sponsor. Maybe Quicksilver? Or a local company like Hawai'ian Island Creations would be nice. The really big guys wouldn't care about him because he was so young, but if he did well enough, they might watch him for the future.

His stomach growled and he wished he'd eaten more breakfast. The plate lunch trucks weren't open yet, but the smell of rice cooking was tantalizing.

Despite the humidity, the sand was cool and the sun barely peeked over the Ko'olau mountains. Lots of shade. He'd better pick a board and—

"Oh, shit." He'd promised not to go near the sponsor house. How could he get a board if he didn't go there?

"Dis just gets bettah and bettah." He plopped in the sand to think. Judging by the sun and lack of people, he had hours before Alani showed up. If he didn't surf in the morning heats, he had a long day of nothing. He didn't dare leave the beach since the way the previous days had gone, the schedule changed in a flash. He would not risk losing his shot. He felt this was a turning point for him. He was doing well, but not well enough to secure a spot if he missed today's ride. The main contest was scheduled to start this weekend. Tomorrow. He prayed to be included.

Things changed so fast, he thought. Before, he was just happy to be here. Ride a few giant waves, get a feel for things, work for his future in professional surfing. Now in a matter of days his rides had improved exponentially. Eldon gone.

Aliki missed his ride. A couple other guys out due to injuries. Not life threatening, but a few torn muscles from bad falls off massive waves—enough to eliminate them. All these pieces led to him sitting pretty, smack at the bottom of the pack, but *in* the pack none the less. Felt great. Terrifying. He was starting to get wound up. He remembered to breathe like Auntie said.

"Hey!" Kahana dropped onto the sand next to him.

Startled, his breath whooshed out. "Hey," he managed.

"Crazy day, yesterday, yeah?"

"Yeah, crazy."

"You hear about Eldon? He's on your team, yeah? You must have heard. He's dead!"

"Yeah, I know," Raj said weakly.

"What happened? Everyone's saying he O.D.'d."

"I don't know what happened." The coconut telegraph was alive and well but he didn't want to correct her because in ten seconds everyone would know he was involved. Sort of involved.

"You ever see him do any drugs?"

"No. I've seen him surf for years. He looked healthy to me, but you nevah know."

"Yeah, I, I mean, we—me and Dylan—try to be healthy, but some a dese guys surf all day and drink beer and smoke *pakalolo* all night. You can't be a pro li' dat. Right?" He nodded and she kept going. "I know some of these guys do more than weed, but not the real athletes." She spoke with authority. "You t'ink he was dealing? That can get you in trouble."

"I don't know. I didn't really know him." But Raj knew from years with his Auntie that people did all kinds of things that were bad for them and that no one else expected them to do.

"I guess it could be ice. I hear some guys use it." She fell silent.

Raj was so far out of the drug world that beyond knowing the basics, weed, coke and the big H, he was at a loss. He'd heard about mushrooms, and for a while, wouldn't eat anything with mushrooms on it 'til his buddies at school educated him. He also knew about pills, but not which ones did what. When he had his wisdom teeth pulled they gave him some narcotic pain meds and that made him pukey and 'stupid' according to his sister, Justine. Ice? That was a new one for him.

This whole conversation was bringing him down. All he knew was Eldon was dead and drug-related or not, that had altered his own status on the team. He needed to prepare and Kahana, although well-meaning, was a distraction.

"Kahana! There you are," her brother Dylan said. "We been looking for you. Come, let's go to our spot before some tourist gets it. Hey, Raj. Howzit?"

Grateful for the interruption, Raj stood and hand-slapped Dylan. "Good brah, good. How you?"

"Excellent. Yesterday, trippy, huh?"

"For shua."

"You still no get one board? Or it stashed someplace?" He laughed. "Your orange monster got ate, yeah? So glad I nevah saw dat shark."

Raj didn't mention he'd been in the water with it. "Yeah, yeah. No board. My sponsor house closed now. Crime scene you know. No board yet."

"Where your sponsor, brah?" Dylan looked around.

"Bad Boyz Beach, but I nevah see him yet."

"You see da line up? You early, brah. Waves is good, so you like break 'em!"

"Early? I gotta see," Raj said.

"Hey, you can use my board again. You brought me luck when I surfed with it afters!" Dylan called.

"T'anks, eh. I check da lineup and den I get your board. I owe you man." Raj sped over to the posting. The crowd had swelled considerably while Kahana had been filling his head with stories of drugs and death. The sun was high enough to leave a line of gold along the sand from the crest of the rise to the ocean that glowed like a welcome carpet. His ride was soon and they had changed into three man heats for this advanced level.

His heart thumped with excitement. The humidity had dropped and he pulsed with energy. But it was a little different. It was a controlled energy and for the first time since he got here, he felt he belonged.

He raced to where Dylan's crew had hung out yesterday. They were there, but the group had swelled.

143

"Hey, dere's da guy who make my board lucky!" Dylan yelled out.

Raj blushed but even this low-level notoriety made him feel good. "Nah, nah, nah." He flapped his hands in the island negative.

Introductions were made with much hand slapping and good wishes. Dylan handed over the board after an abbreviated Hawai'ian blessing and Kahana surprised him with a peck on the cheek.

"Good luck out there," she said. "Be safe, we'll be watching out for you!"

"T'anks, eh. Wish me luck. See you afters."

Raj took the board with him back to the lineup posting. Not too much time to wait. He was handed a blue jersey. Still no sign of Jet or Aliki. Could use some advice right now. He wished Jet had filled him in. Maybe had something to do with Eldon. Maybe Jet was being investigated. Best not to think about that.

Other than Kahana and her brother, Raj felt very alone. He hadn't bonded with the team. It was not unusual. He hadn't spent any time with them and he hadn't stayed at the team house. Just as well, given the circumstances. But his insecurity made him feel extremely isolated. His practice and training were all he had. His Auntie was his best friend out here. His parents didn't really understand, although they supported him as best they could. Even his dad had surprised him when he'd overheard a conversation which told him they hoped he'd go to college 'once this surfing thing' got out of his system. Justine had her own life, and although the folks thought she was going to college, he knew Justine was considering a career in the Coast Guard. Good luck to their parents. That made him smile.

The sun glowed on the waves now. Things warmed up and the familiar sound of air horn bleats and heat announcements comforted him. He waxed his borrowed lucky board and gathered with the other surfers. The heats had changed in that they were no longer color-grouped. Each surfer had a different color in these heats. He stretched out to relieve his nerves and then focused on the waves and the performance of other surfers.

Above the Pipe the sun was bright, but the darkness to the west inched forward. He hoped the pace stayed the same so everyone got his ride in. If the qualifying heats were delayed, much less the final contest, his nerves would not last, frayed as they were.

So far, he'd managed to block out Eldon Hayashi's death, but suddenly Eldon was on his mind. Maybe it was drugs. Maybe he O.D.'d like Kahana speculated or fell and hit his head. His inner voice told him that was not the case. *Dead bodies did not crawl under beds. But maybe, he was disoriented and crawled under to die? That was possible, right? Don't think about it. Just don't.*

The horn sounded the end of the previous heat; Myles Freeh, and two other guys, probably lower in standing. However, they all had great rides and he knew from watching hours of video their scores would be close by tenths or even hundredths.

He readied to paddle out. All he hoped for was a decent finish without making an idiot of himself. An eternity of waiting. The horn. He started paddling. He looked to see who was in his heat. Aliki. How was that possible? And another guy he didn't know. Yes, he did. Eric Lee. Weird that all three of them were BBB guys. Eric Lee was excellent, but not at the top. He was a really great guy by all accounts, but couldn't rise above Aliki until now. Eric hadn't said much at the meeting, he was known to be a quiet guy. In fact, although he took all the good natured ribbing from the team, he mostly concentrated on his video tape. He was the only guy Raj saw that took notes. Raj pondered the meaning of that and got a wave in the face.

He paddled against increasing pressure. A set built and the sky darkened. The wave was too close and he let it pass but the promised storm was arriving. He hoped it would be later rather than sooner. Raj so wanted to be a part of this world, he could taste it. An overwhelming yearning and steel filled him. From not having a chance at all, just being a spectator really, to having a shot at professional competition. He wished he'd paid more attention to the weather forecast. Too much on his mind. Eldon's lop-sided face on the gurney flashed in his brain and he had to slam a door to stop the image.

Between the waves was not a slow build but a quick chop, like rapids for kayaks. He straddled his board, trying to judge his best approach. Aliki was too close. Raj moved away, but Aliki trailed.

Raj was in the water with a murderer. Well, maybe he was. He made himself stop thinking about it.

Eric watched the slow motion chase but stayed away. Raj saw him flash a compassionate expression but he was ready for a wave. A swell built far out. It would be amazing by the time it came into range. Raj paddled away but again, Aliki dogged him. He thought Aliki wasn't trying to catch anything, but only mess up a ride for Raj. Probably. But Raj knew he was the better surfer now and probably the better person. He gauged the wave. Still far but getting huge. No curl yet. No foam except the line of frosting along the crest.

Raj waited until the last moment. He paddled toward the wave and behind Aliki. Aliki wasn't ready for it, and couldn't adjust. He tried to maneuver but didn't make it and was caught sideways and flipped.

Raj had planned well. He stroked and felt the familiar lift—that moment at the top frozen before the wave let go and rolled over. All other thoughts flew away and he just rode. His board skimmed and sailed, up down, in out, arms out in balance and symmetry. He carved out a 360 as he dropped down and back up, his fin lifting when he hit the lip of the wave and he rotated his shoulders. He stayed coiled over the back of his board and released his momentum to complete the turn. His hand brushed the pewter wall reflected in the sky. Or maybe it was the other way around. Shafts of sunlight lit the dark sky and penetrated the gray like spotlights. The usually green wall was dark and the only light was the exit. He put both hands out to reach the sides of the tunnel and a stab of fear and adrenaline coursed through him as he felt a solid shape surf the wave with him. He knew exactly what it was.

He remembered to breathe. He kept calm. His knees were weak but he held on. He prayed to hold on, now for his life more than for a winning ride.

The sun brightened as he left the tunnel and the wave opened up, letting him sail toward the beach. The main part of the wave was done, yet had enough push that he still surfed at least twenty feet above the flat water. He rode out, keeping his weight under him toward the tail of the board. He risked a glance back and saw Eric had caught the next wave and was doing well. No sign of Aliki.

The horn sounded but he would have come back in anyway. He was almost afraid to drop down after the wave crumbled. His heart had settled a little and he scanned the water for the shark he'd seen a few moments ago.

Dozens of people were in the water and no one looked upset. The rescue teams, surf photographers, boats, surfers, it was a busy place. Nothing. Hadn't anyone else seen the shark?

I can't be a surfer if I'm scared of the water. Or rather, what's in the water, he amended. The ocean was their home. He was a guest. He'd seen sharks before, but black tips, white tips, lemons, all the places he'd surfed had sharks, but he'd never seen a Tiger until this contest. And he'd never seen anything this big, never this close, and it scared him.

Eric was right behind him coming up the beach, jubilant with his good ride as well. They exchanged a smile and headed toward the score board.

Raj forgot about Aliki as his little 'fan club' clapped him on the back and complimented his excellent run.

Time for a break and some food. Raj also forgot about meeting Alani and headed to the food trucks to eat with Kahana, Dylan and the group he now considered friends.

Time flew and the heats were over by the time they finished lunch. He was grateful for the companionship of Kahana, Dylan and their friends, but as they parted he got a good look at the sky and his surroundings.

The wind was up and the contest was shutting down. He checked the judge's stand. No Alani. He was sure it was afternoon by the glimpses of blurry sun amid the gray. People bustled about battening down the hatches. A coconut leaf hat rolled by in the wind like a tumbleweed in a bad western movie.

Raj was uneasy. He waited by the boards and although he was thrilled that his ride had gotten him in the contest, that faded as he scanned the emptying beach for the familiar figure of Alani. Maybe he was late? Auntie gave him a cell phone number to call.

Shoots, I forget 'em, he scolded himself. The parking lot was almost empty and no bright orange squashed Papaya car. He dragged out the paper with the phone number and it was damp.

Nearly illegible. *Shoots. Maybe can call Auntie? No, she's in court. And she doesn't have a cell phone yet.* He'd been working on her to get one, but hadn't succeeded yet.

The last food truck drove away and he felt really alone. *Maybe I can call Alani's house and he'll check his messages?* He lifted the pay phone receiver only to find the phone was broken. *Great. Cannot even call 911 or collect.*

The school! Auntie said the school was still in session. He quickly crossed the lot and trotted down the road a bit to Sunset Beach Elementary. No cars remained in the lot. Either it was later than he thought, or they'd closed school early because of the storm.

Double shoots. Fat rain drops hit the pavement and quickly escalated. He'd check one more time at the judges' stand, but after that, he really didn't know what else to do. He was not going to stand in the rain waiting for Alani.

Back at the deserted stand he was completely alone. The waves were huge and angry, pounding the short beach and threatening to wash over the multi-story structure. It shook in the wind and Raj needed to find shelter off the beach. He didn't have a choice, so he headed for the sponsor house. At least there would be cops there since it was a crime scene, Auntie said. Maybe one of them—the detective maybe—could find out where she was or how long she'd be. The North Shore had never felt alien to him, but the weather made it frightening; foreign and isolated.

The beach side route, although potentially more dangerous, was half the time it would take to go around the block to the front. He put his head down and ran along the houses. Even this far up the beach, his feet got wet in swirling storm surge. He wondered how long it would be until it reached the homes. Maybe this was a full-on hurricane. He didn't know; he'd been so out of touch all day. Auntie wouldn't worry because she thought Alani was here. Something might have happened to Alani and he'd not been able to tell either him or Auntie. What a mess.

He reached the back gate and all was quiet. The patio door was locked. *Makes sense, everybody inside cuz dis crappy weather,* he grumbled. He used his old trick of bumping the slider off the track to get in when no one answered his knock. *Probably can't hear cuz da noise from da storm.* Which was considerable, now that he was paying attention. He didn't really want to run into a cop while breaking in, but at this point, he'd settle for any human, no matter how pissed off.

He flipped the light switch and nothing happened. "Well, das jus' great." No power. That meant no phones, either.

The storm threw palm fronds and coconuts all over the beach. He looked out the slider for a moment and a coconut flew straight as a missile at him where he stood behind the glass. He didn't have time to react, but the wind lifted it and sailed it harmlessly over the house.

"Jeez!" Raj's heart pounded and he backed away from the door. He tried the phone anyway, but of course, with no electricity, it didn't work. Despite the noise, the house was too quiet. Too quiet to be filled with detectives or crime scene guys. *Whatevers. Maybe they done? Maybe the storm cause problems so dey investigating someplace else?*

At any rate, he felt a bit safer indoors. No one would find him here, but he worried that maybe Alani would be looking for him. He made a mental note to check the parking lot again later. He sat at the dining table, away from the glass and watched, fascinated as the storm ripped the shore apart.

A rustling and bumping made its way into his subconscious. He realized someone was upstairs. Great! Maybe someone collecting evidence he didn't hear earlier. They would have a radio thing and could call someone. Or a car. He could get home. *Alani would probably just leave if he couldn't find me,* he rationalized. Right now all he wanted was to be off the North Shore as soon as possible.

Torrential rain sheeted the windows and he could no longer see out. He went upstairs and the noise stopped. He headed to the master bedroom since he knew that's where the crime scene was.

"Hey," he called. Nothing. He popped his head in but didn't see anyone with tweezers. He smiled grimly to himself. "Anybody here? I kinda stuck heah on my own. Can use a ride or your walkie-talkie?"

He turned back and opened the next bedroom door. Robert Goto held a stack of perforated dot-matrix computer paper, the accordioned sheets flowing from his hands to the floor where he had dropped them.

Raj was so shocked it wasn't a cop he just stood there. "Um, hi. What are you doing here? I thought this was closed?"

"Yeah. It is closed. What are you doing here?" Goto asked.

"I got stuck up here with no ride. My ride stay late and my Auntie, she no can . . ." Raj drifted into pidgin and then stopped. Something clicked in his brain. What was it?

Goto's shoes. They were brand new. A style BBB had recently brought out and had given to its team members to try. Neon colors. Now Raj remembered the meeting at the hotel. Just about everybody, Jet, Goto, Eric wore the signature shoes. He'd wondered if he would get a pair. Each had a different color. But that's not what really clicked for Raj. He'd seen the shoes someplace else.

Goto knew it too. The shoes, with feet still in them, were in the master bedroom closet where Goto was hiding when Raj looked for his board. That's what was wrong. The shoes didn't seem empty at the time, because they weren't. Raj hadn't paid any attention because he'd been so upset about his board.

"You killed him? You killed Eldon? And he was under the bed when I—"

Goto dropped the papers and lunged at Raj who turned and darted out of the bedroom and down the stairs. He had nowhere to go, and no idea where he *could* go, but he wasn't going to stay here. He jerked open the front door and raced down the slate path to the turtle gate. A moment of panic when the gate stuck gave Goto a chance to catch up. Raj ran into the little street, partially shielded by the jungle and overhanging ironwood trees. He didn't know the area well. He didn't live here, only came to surf. Up until this year, he couldn't drive, and like all kids, paid no attention to how he got somewhere, just that it was where he wanted to go.

He pounded down the street toward the parking lot of Ehukai Beach Park, the landing zone for Pipeline. All the houses were set back from the street like the team rental house. He had no idea if they were occupied and he was terrified of getting trapped. Goto had killed once to hide something, and Raj didn't doubt he would be next. Easy to disguise his own hit over the head as a blow from a fallen branch. No one would ever know. Maybe he'd 'drown,' a casualty of the storm.

Right now he wished he hadn't watched so much *Law & Order* with his Auntie. He also wished he hadn't eavesdropped on her case discussions. Further, he wished he was at home with her right now eating grilled cheese watching a bad movie with Teresa between them.

Surfing gave him excellent stamina and he regained his lead over Goto. But he didn't keep it. Instead of feet pounding after him, he heard the roar of a big engine and glanced back to see a black over red Mustang pull out from under the shelter of the ironwood trees. He couldn't outrun a car.

He thought he was imagining things when he saw the Papaya sitting in the lot. The rain was a wall and he was sure he was wrong, but the closer he ran, the more solid it became. No Alani. He yelled, but he couldn't hear his own voice over the rain. He felt more than heard the big V8 engine behind him. Goto must have thought he was trapped since he didn't just run him down. *Harder to make like one accident, maybe?* he thought.

Nevermind. He yanked open the driver's door of the Papaya, remembering that nothing locked on this car.

"Keys please, Alani, keys please," he chanted as he felt around under the threadbare floor mat. He felt the surfer key bob and then it began to slip out of a rust hole in the floor. He grabbed it back as it slithered forward.

He jammed the key in the ignition and, for all its physical faults, the Papaya tried to start but immediately stalled since it was in gear. "Shit, come on, you!" Raj plunged in the clutch and cranked the engine over. He threw it into first and almost stalled again popping the clutch. He rammed it in again, the engine roaring as momentum kept the car moving. He cranked the wheel toward the exit and heard his Auntie's voice in his head, "Just breathe."

He accelerated until the engine whined, still in first, and he gulped a big breath as he struggled for second and lurched out onto Kam highway. Hands clenched on the wheel, sweat sliding off the gear shift, he shoved it into third. The back window was completely fogged but he was sure the big Mustang followed him. What was he thinking? He had nowhere to go; only now he was in a car he could barely drive and could go maybe 50 miles per hour tops. Great getaway car. Great plan.

He could hardly see the road but all he could think to do was hide. A bright orange, smashed up Papaya car. *Yeah, dat would blend in perfectly.* He could keep going but he knew the road from traveling in the last big storm. He did not want to wash into the ocean and have it do the job for Goto. He knew he could not outrun the Mustang. He kept the pedal to the metal and saw the access road for ComSat coming up. He'd opened the window so the condensation had dissipated, and although he wasn't sure through the downpour, he now thought he'd lost the Mustang in the curves. He swerved off Kam highway onto the road that led to the satellite installation. He downshifted to keep his speed on the turn and through the slight grade as it rose above the main road.

The access road was not long enough. Once through the trees it was ramrod straight with no cover. He kept going. Maybe Goto'd miss the turn. Or maybe he would keep going, thinking Raj was ahead, until there were too many places he *could* have turned off for him to check.

Raj reached the locked gate surrounding the facility itself. The days of rain had made the grassy plain surrounding the installation a mud hole. One tire in there and he'd never get out. No place to hide. He turned the car on the tarmac, faced out and waited.

*   *   *   *

K.O. sat on the hard wood bench outside the courtroom. She'd testified once, but would be called back again. She didn't want to leave and further draw out this super fun day if she left and they had to look for her. She had risked a quick run to the coffee cart down the hall, but now she was paying for it. The ladies room was even farther away, around a corner and with her luck, she knew she'd be called the second she was in there.

She was in the old court building downtown, behind the statue of King Kamehameha. Windows extended to the ceiling. The hall had gotten darker and darker as she'd sat there. Finally, court broke for lunch and she still hadn't testified.

She spoke to the bailiff. After the pleasantries she asked, "I'm wondering if I'm going to get called again today. I know you can't tell me what's going on specifically, but what chu t'ink, brah?"

"Between you and me, no. But not because da case. I hear we on hurricane watch and we might cancel after lunch. Dey goin' decide at lunch. Da waves is crazy on da Nort' Shore, I heah."

K.O.'s stomach dropped. "Yeah? Like what? Any news?"

"What's wrong?"

"My nephew, he stay up dere for Pipeline, you know? He qualifying today and I couldn't get out a dis." She gestured to the courtroom.

"Oh, man. You should go. My seestah stay up in Waialua and dey puttin' up dere plywood li' dat."

Jerry referred to the nailing up of plywood all over doors, windows, sliders and louvers—any glass—that could shatter during a storm. Waialua was the next town over from Haleiwa and anything happening there was surely happening all along that coast.

Panic welled up in K.O. "Jerry, he's only fifteen. My boyfriend was supposed to be up there with him, but I haven't been able to get a hold of him either. You think they cancelled the trials?"

"Fo' shua. Everybody getting ready for dis to turn into Iniki or somet'ing. Dey said one storm, but dis turning out to be like one hurricane, you know?"

Back then, during hurricane Iniki, K.O. had been called out, like all of HPD as well as the fire department. What a mess. And terrifying. She'd been heading to a call and driving on the H-1 freeway, lakes of rain to plow through and her patrol car had literally lifted off the pavement for a second or two at a time the whole way. All she could think of was the wind whipping up at the wrong moment and her car flying and flipping off the raised freeway. She shivered at the memory. The islands still hadn't fully recovered from Iniki, and now this?

"Jerry, I gotta go. My nephew, he could be all alone up there. You said court's gonna be postponed. If it's not, make something up for me, yeah? I got sick or something."

"You look pretty sick to me, girl."

K.O. didn't mind the diminutive nickname coming from Jerry. He was a silver-haired, shoulda-retired-already court bailiff who was always kind to her.

"I *feel* sick. I don't know how long it's gonna take me to get there. An hour in good conditions, and now, if everybody tries to move inland at the same time . . ."

"Hey." Jerry put a big hand on her shoulder. "He gon' be fine. You'll see. Da surfer guys, dey stick together. He at someone's house right now playing spin da bottle wit' some cute surfer *wahine*. Try wait."

K.O. smiled, knowing he was trying to make her feel better. "T'anks, eh." She gave him a quick hug and took off at a run for the parking garage.

As she pulled into traffic, rain pelted down bringing visibility to near zero. Cars lined bumper to bumper as everyone tried to get out of downtown. Nimitz Highway, near the harbor, paralleled the core, and although it was a main thoroughfare, folks were leaving the waterfront area and funneling into the already jammed downtown. She tried to be patient and used the time to plan her route. Could leave downtown on Nu'uanu and be on the Pali Highway north. That was closer, but not necessarily quicker, since tons of people doing that. She would also have a long drive from Kailua to Pipeline on the ocean side of the skinny road. No thanks. She wended her way toward the Pali and sure enough, Nu'uanu was a parking lot. She inched west onto Vineyard and figured Likelike Highway would be the same and she'd have the same issue. Getting to the windward side would only mean a long and hazardous drive right next to

159

the ocean. Or maybe impassable by the time she got there and all her planning would be for nothing since she'd be stranded and unable to get to Raj. That was the problem with having only one road to get someplace.

Frustrated, she turned on the radio, trying to get a weather report. She also turned up her police radio. Maybe she could offset some traffic issues if she had a clue. She tuned to KPOI, her favorite rock station, and it was business as usual. She let it play to calm her nerves and hoped a bulletin would air between songs. *Can't be too bad if we're not on high alert, right? They would blast the emergency sirens if*—in answer to her thoughts, the sirens cut through and broke into the song. Sure enough, Harry Kim, the head of civil defense, outlined the current situation and listed options depending on where people were on the island, and on which island.

Traffic got worse as people fled low-lying areas. She was already past the onramps for Waikiki, but she'd been on duty before when they'd tried to evacuate either terrified or nonchalant tourists. Nothing bad happens when you're on vacation, right? Ahhh. So frustrating. And you had to be nice to them.

The police band heated up with traffic accidents, issues of elderly and infirm citizens. Calls of flooding and panic. All the while the rain never stopped. The car lifted and rocked and her adrenaline spiked, instantly taking her back to Iniki even though this was nothing like that.

"Just breathe," she said aloud. She said it again for her and for Raj and felt a little better. She edged past the exit for Likelike and the freeway opened up a bit as it neared the airport exits. Again, she considered heading north on the H-3, if only to get out of this mess. Rational thought prevailed and she stuck it out. It took her an hour to get to the H-2 northbound ramp. Traffic had not lessened, but people were driving better. She saw a slow migration of traffic moving from the coastal flats to the center of the island, Waipahu, Mililani, and into the valleys.

She raced along H-2 at 30 miles an hour or so in heavy traffic. As she got closer to Wahiawa and the interesting turns needed to get to Haleiwa and the north shore, the traffic switched up and started coming toward her. These folks were also fleeing the coast but from the north down.

H-2 faded into 80 where it had become a two-lane mud-caked parking lot. Heavy rains washed red dirt from the cane and pineapple fields onto the road and drivers weren't sure where to go. Drainage ditches filled with muddy water looked like part of the road and mired vehicles attested to their mistakes. K.O. turned on her blue light and called for tow wagons. She felt obliged to stop and check for injuries and give directions for staying safe in this weather. She was able to pull to the side and get out her rain gear. At one point she left her vehicle and walked car to car. The delay ate at her, but she saw the panic and fear on the faces and hoped someone would do that for Raj if he was scared. She worried she might get run over with visibility at nil, but with so many cars stopped, the worry waned as she did her job. She helped a few cars nose out of the wrong lane and encouraged drivers to continue on to get out of the way. A raised dually truck with a tow package stopped to help stuck drivers. She went over to thank the driver and was a little surprised to see a gigantic Samoan or Tongan man, tatted up for days with huge muscles and a helmet of soggy, frizzy, black hair, gently urging a tiny Japanese woman to stay in her car and keep dry while he took care of her. *You just never know the kindness of strangers.* Reminder for herself about judging books and covers.

The need to find Raj was intense and only growing so she left the scene after radioing an update and thanking the truck driver. Another hour had past. She edged the Crown Vic, blue bubble whirling, along highway 80 until it met 99 by the pineapple garden. Finally she felt she was getting somewhere.

She sped up to 45 until she hit Haleiwa but stayed on the bypass to save time. Past the town she had to slow again as the road neared the ocean and continued into the curves around Waimea Bay. The huge rock in the bay was a nub as storm surge crashed into it and washed into the estuary. Enough water was diffused to allow road access, but it was not an easy or pretty trip for K.O. Traversing this same route eight hours ago had been a completely different journey.

With great relief she came off the cliffs past Waimea and onto the flats where the good winter surf spots were. She didn't recognize any of it. If not for the signs proclaiming the different beach parks, she would have had no idea where she was.

Ghost towns greeted her. No traffic. No people. Not even the ubiquitous dogs. Ironwood trees dropped needles in the swirling winds, but K.O. was grateful for their huge and sturdy-looking trunks between her and the ocean. She worried for the houses along the beach and hoped everyone escaped to the highlands, if not out of the area. Sharp green mountain spires rose on the inland side and between those and the storm she felt trapped and alone.

She lowered her speed and swung her head from side to side, looking, wishing, for something. Some sign. *Ridiculous. He's not going to be standing out here all alone with his thumb out waiting.*

A bubble of panic. Where should she go? She couldn't leave without him. How on Earth would she find him? Should she knock on doors? Or pray. It didn't look like a populated area but she knew there were hundreds of homes tucked among the hills and trees. People helped each other in disasters. He could have been invited into a home anywhere and she'd never find him until the storm stopped. Or, he could be lost or hurt. She had no idea what kind of panic had ensued up here when the storm turned dangerous. She had counted on Alani and now she couldn't reach him. Maybe Raj was with Alani after all and he was fine. She should have called Alani's house before she left the courthouse. From her radio she knew that all electricity was out from Waialua to Kahaluu and more communities would probably be down before it was over. She hadn't seen any Hawai'ian Electric trucks out. They were always out, so if they couldn't make it, no one could.

What if Raj had been lost in the shuffle? What if he'd been in the water and hurt, knocked unconscious or just abandoned? Jet was useless and that stupid house chaperone . . . the house. She should check the house. She'd told Raj not to go there, but if he had nowhere to go and no one to help him, he might have gone there. She'd said it was a crime scene, so he might have gone there looking for help.

Relieved to have a plan, she poked along looking for the turnout. She almost missed it and stopped in the road deciding if it was the right one. It looked completely different. Most of the shrubbery was stripped and since she'd never seen a street sign before, seeing one now wasn't a big help. She envisioned the turn into the little street relative to the beach parking lot and proximity to Sunset Beach Elementary. The other place she'd told him to go, but now that was pointless.

She pulled in and looked for the turtle gate. Got it. Again, she almost missed it because the yard was a garden of leafless sticks. The wall was the same, but the gate was open so she didn't see the turtle at first.

She exited her car and the wind about knocked her over. She tried calling out, but her words were swept away. She fought her way up the slate walk. The front door was open, the foyer soaked from windblown rain. Not good.

She drew her Glock .26 and walked cautiously through the downstairs. She couldn't help the rustle her rain gear made, but the noise of the storm might mask that. Her nerves jangled and she hesitated calling out. If Raj was hiding, so be it. She'd find him. If someone else was hiding, she didn't want to give him or her an advantage.

No sign of anyone or anything different downstairs. She poked open all the downstairs doors. Nothing. Staying to the wall side of the stairway to reduce creaks, she crept up. She always hated that moment when her head was higher than her body ascending a staircase. So vulnerable. She crouched as much as possible to reduce her head being a spectacular target, but her precautions were for nothing. She checked the bathroom, closets, and made her way to the master bedroom—the main crime scene. The bed had been dismembered and a large square of carpet removed from under it where the body had bled. The closet doors were open and no one was inside. Her heart settled a bit as her anxiety receded.

She pushed open the last door to another bedroom. A pile of connected perforated printer sheets lay in a jumble on the floor. That wasn't there before. She'd have seen it, and if it was evidence, it would have been removed with everything else. She checked the closet and under the bed. No one. She turned her attention to the papers.

Financial documents, and a lot of them. Bad Boyz Beach papers. A couple disconnected sheets, emails from Jet to Goto. Apparently, not only was Goto the world's worst house chaperone, he was also the financial head of BBB. Scanning the emails, Jet wanted the company to go public which K.O. gathered meant being on the New York Stock Exchange. Beyond her monthly contribution to her police pension, K.O. knew nothing of the stock market or investments. She read quickly, keeping one ear open for non-storm noise.

Jet asked Goto to get documents ready for the IPO. More scanning. *The Initial Public Offering.* Jet wanted Goto to pull all the financials for an investment banking firm who would check it all before underwriting it. Them. It was getting confusing. Jet said that the investment bank would then put together a registration statement to be filed with the SEC. *What?* Securities and Exchange Commission. Government money guys. That was fairly straightforward, but K.O.'s head was starting to hurt. She set down the emails and picked up the accordion sheets.

Now she got really confused. A bunch of numbers in columns, incoming money, outgoing money. That made sense but a lot of abbreviations didn't. Something else was curious. Names and dates were identical in two areas, but the money numbers were different. K.O. wished she'd paid more attention during Math class in school.

Her gut told her this was important and since it was here now, but not before, that was also significant. It did not, however, get her any closer to finding Raj. She gathered everything up quickly and stuffed it under her rain gear. She was satisfied she was alone in the house, but needed to get moving.

She dashed back to her car, closing the front door and gate. She drove back to the parking lot of the contest, just in case. Banners flapped sadly, half torn from their moorings, the welcome arch sagged and branches and rubbish whisked by in the wind.

She pulled out onto Kam Highway and continued south slowly, looking.

Suddenly, all was still, alarming in its abruptness. She'd experienced the eye of the storm before during hurricanes Iwa and Iniki. A feeling of calm and relief that it was over, but it wasn't really. Only a bubble of calm sandwiched between all hell breaking loose.

In the moments of no rain, no wind and near silence, she saw a car coming toward her in the distance. The first car in forever. Her alarm bells went off. A Mustang, black vinyl top over cherry red, turned south on the ComSat road. It didn't hesitate; it seemed deliberate, which further tightened her gut.

Her silver Crown Vic, rain colored, cloud colored, storm colored, was invisible at this distance. She hoped. Her police light had been turned off since she stopped at the house. She made the turn after the car. She stayed well back, the feeling of dread increasing. The Mustang was out of sight in the curves, but K.O. knew there was no way out. The road dead-ended at the satellite installation. She had no idea what was happening, but sure it was nothing good. No employee would be out here, and certainly not in a personal vehicle.

She came out of the curves and headed up the straight incline to the gate. At the top, in the flat parking area, she was shocked to see the Mustang facing the Papaya. She stopped her car and the driver of the Mustang got out. Goto. She heard its big engine running in the silence, over her Crown Vic, in the void inside the storm.

*   *   *   *

Raj knew it was only a matter of time before Robert found him. He'd hidden as best he could, but even with the length of time it took for Goto to check the roads south of here, he knew he'd be discovered. He had not come up with a plan in all that time. He was smaller, skinnier, younger and not nearly as desperate as the man who hunted him. He was out of options.

When Raj saw the Mustang come up the road, he turned on the Papaya's engine, thinking to out maneuver him—somehow getting around him. But Goto was too fast and skidded the Mustang in front of him. Raj had not left enough room behind the Papaya. He was too close to the chain link fence to back up.

The storm had stopped and the complete stillness freaked him out after hours of noise. It had become a sort of comfort, the crash and boom, the pressure of the atmosphere, the heaviness of the rain and violence of the wind. Now its absence was a distraction, he was hyper-aware, waiting for something.

Goto got out of the driver's seat carrying a tire iron. Raj knew it was for him, and that his 'accident' might never be discovered to be the murder it was. He couldn't run, he couldn't fight. Raj's terror leapt into his throat as he waited.

*   *   *   *

K.O. watched helplessly as Goto got out of the Mustang holding a tire iron. Her reactions were a little delayed from seeing the Papaya in a place it never should have been. She stepped on the gas, but by the time her car reached the Mustang, it was over.

*   *   *   *

Raj didn't think at all. He didn't plan it. He put the Papaya in gear and it lurched forward once and died. Raj waited but nothing happened. Out of his peripheral vision he saw someone running toward him and he threw his hands up in front of his face. He couldn't take anymore.

"It's okay, it's okay." His Auntie's voice. How could that be? She was in court. In Honolulu. "Come on, get out." She helped him out of the car and held him tight. She tried to shield him with her body, but he saw. He'd hit Robert Goto and crushed him between the two cars. The tire iron lay inches from Goto's hand.

"Sit in my car." She guided him to the plush, dry Crown Vic and handed him a drink of water from her mug. He threw it up immediately on the parking area.

"It's okay, it's okay," she said over and over. "Keep your head down for a minute, the dizziness and nausea should pass." She gently pushed his head over his lap. "I'll be right back."

Raj lifted his head enough to see her kneel down next to Goto's body. She returned quickly, holding the tire iron by two fingers in a tissue. She put it in an evidence bag and set it behind the driver's seat. She picked up the radio.

"You didn't kill him, he's alive," she told him, then turned her attention to the radio, calling for back-up, and an ambulance. His attention faded. She put the radio back.

"It's going to be okay. Really. We're going to figure this out. While we wait, can you tell me what happened?"

"I'm so tired Auntie."

"I know." They sat for a moment and the storm sounds began picking up again. "Crap." K.O. got out of the car to retrieve a tarp from her trunk. "Oh, no!"

"What?" Raj called back to her.

"Your board. Still in da trunk. I nevah turn it in to evidence. Great. I'll never make detective at this rate."

"Maybe it's not evidence," Raj said.

"But it might be. That's the point. We don't know for sure. Way to go, Ogden." She removed the tarp, made a little awning between the cars over Robert Goto, and weighed it down as best she could from more junk from the trunk. She leaned in Raj's window.

"If I had to take a guess, I think he used the tire iron," Raj said and sipped more water. He kept it down this time.

"I think so too, but procedure, brah. Let's hope. If Keahi wants to complain I ruined the crime scene with the tarp, let 'em. I tried."

Raj smiled a little. "Crime scene, huh?"

"Yeah. You were amazing. I'd better stay with Goto though. I don't want to, but I'd better."

Raj was relieved that he didn't have to talk to her. For now.

*   *   *   *

K.O. got an umbrella and sat next to Goto. She tried to remain professional, but thinking of Goto smashing her most precious Raj, the way he'd killed Eldon Hayashi, someone else's son or brother, made her so angry she shook.

Goto rasped each breath, but he continued to live. The only reason she was relieved was that Raj wouldn't face a manslaughter charge at some point. Her thoughts were disjointed, but she let them sift as they would. She went through lawyers in her mental Rolodex. George for sure. He was the best one she knew. Raj acted in self-defense, but she was going to get the best. From what she'd read of those printouts, Goto was definitely fiddling BBB's books, but how did that lead to Eldon being dead? She hoped she'd preserved the tire iron well enough since Goto might have used that on him. Why?

171

The books would take a forensic accountant to decode, but perhaps they weren't related? Maybe Eldon was killed to let someone else move up in the BBB ranks. Aliki was the most likely suspect, but that had backfired because he'd missed an important heat, plus his surfing was way below par. Raj had made the cut and if he'd surfed well today, this morning—so long ago—he'd qualified for the contest itself. She should ask. She leaned against the Mustang and propped the umbrella between her knees.

Sirens broke into her thoughts. She didn't move. They'd find her soon enough. Her job was to protect Raj.

The storm came back in earnest. In the cold wind and rain, she got even colder remembering that she was going to have to tell her sister at some point. Probably soon. That scared her almost as much as worrying about Raj.

She was relieved to see Keahi's cranky face when he got out of his car. The devil she knew. She motioned for Raj to stay in her car.

The desolate site was soon filled with sirens, police cars, ambulance, bustle. She gave her statement to Keahi, happy that SIS investigator Jeanine was on call again.

"You again," Jeanine joked. "This your body, too?"

"Nah. This one's my nephew's." K.O. immediately felt bad but humor was a relief too, after the pent up tension.

"Runs in the family, then?" Jeanine's bright blonde hair and sparkling eyes were a little beacon

172

of light. K.O. didn't know how she always seemed so happy, but over a cup of coffee once she mentioned that it gave her pleasure to help find justice for grieving families and that's what kept her ankle deep in disgusting evidence, day after day.

Keahi wanted Raj's statement. She explained she was his legal guardian and would be present. She decided to wait to call the lawyer, depending on how this initial interview went.

She was pleased at Keahi's gentleness. She revised her opinion of him, that maybe he didn't think Raj was a murderer. It was an accident.

Raj would get a ticket for driving without a license and without a driver of legal age present. That had to be documented because of the resulting accident, but K.O. had a feeling that might disappear by the court date.

She was released to take Raj home. By the time they were finished the storm had abated and only sprinkles and gray clouds gave any indication of the storm. That and the utter destruction of the trees. The Papaya was towed to town for evidence. Alani might not be happy, but she would pay any fines. Alani! Where was he?

She drove toward Kaneohe, but stopped at the first pay phone by a bus stop. Raj had said the beach park pay phone was broken. They probably all were by now with the storm. Or maybe Hawai'ian Tel had gotten them back even if Hawai'ian Electric was out.

The phone was no good. Alani was an adult and a local boy. He had friends and had probably figured out a way home. She only wished she knew.

Broken branches littered the wet highway. Storm surge had receded so she could see where she was going. Raj didn't offer up any conversation, and she left him to his own thoughts. Utilities trucks were out now, so the world was returning to normal.

As they neared Time's market she asked, "Should we stop at the store? Need anything?"

"No. I just want to go home."

She nodded in understanding. She had one more hurdle she needed to discuss. "Raj, this has been an awful day, but we're going to have to call your folks."

"I know."

"I'm not advocating lying, but I will follow your lead on how much you want to tell them right now. Any suggestions?"

"I've been thinking about it, too. I know they follow the contest in the papers and they will know about the storm. Everybody will know about that. I don't like to lie, but it might come out that a surfer on my team was killed. What should I say?"

"They don't need to know you were in the room with him, right?"

"Maybe. They're gonna find out that I hit Goto with the Papaya. Won't they?"

"Yes. Maybe. Probably. What if it's some a guy and you, uh, just bumped him when he crossed in front of the car?"

"Where were you? You know my mom's gonna ask that."

"Good point. Maybe I stepped away for a sec?"

"She's gonna kill us."

"Yes, she is." K.O. pulled into her parking spot at the townhouse. Her complex was protected by a range of hills, and the previous storm had knocked out most of the vulnerable branches and bushes already, so it didn't look much different.

"When should we do this?" K.O. unlocked the front door. "Sooner or later?"

"Later. For sure."

They kicked off their shoes and K.O. noticed a pair of large rubber slippers, not hers or Raj's, in the pile.

"Alani!" Raj rushed past her and gave Alani a huge hug.

Alani looked at her over Raj's head. "I didn't know where else to go so I hitched a ride back here to wait." They had exchanged house keys some time ago, given K.O.'s strange work hours and their limited time together.

"What happened to you? I was so worried." K.O. hugged them both. It felt good. Moreover, Raj let them stand like that, all three, together.

"I was late. My shipper didn't pick up on time. The storm made all the pick-ups and deliveries off." K.O. nodded remembering her own struggles in traffic. "I drove up here and the contest was already shut down. The beach pay phone was broken, so I knew Raj couldn't call me. I parked in the lot thinking he'd see the car and wait for me. I waited there for a while, but he didn't come and by then the storm was really crazy. I went to a few nearby houses to see if he was there, but most people had evacuated. I found a guy to give me a ride back. I had no place to go or any way to call you. All the phones and electricity out. I'm so sorry. I figured Raj'd either holed up or gotten a ride out. I left the Papaya just in case, though."

"I'm so glad you did!" Raj released them and plopped into a recliner. Teresa arrived immediately and jumped into his lap. "That car saved my life!"

Alani's eye brows went up. "Yeah? Tell me about it."

K.O. went into the kitchen and popped the tops on three beers. So what? After today, Raj drinking a beer was the least of their problems. She came back and sat on the loveseat since Alani had appropriated the other recliner. She lay back and closed her eyes and listened to Raj recount his harrowing tale. She forced herself to stay quiet and calm, reminding herself that it had all turned out all right. She promised that she would find out what happened, what set of circumstances put all this in motion with Raj in the middle.

Raj's outpouring exhausted him further, but the telling of his adventure seemed to help him. Clarified events. K.O. felt she should tell Raj's parents all was well, but she didn't want to have that conversation yet. As far as they knew, it was only a storm. But as soon as K.O. started talking, Maureen would know it was a shitstorm and K.O. wasn't ready for that. She'd come up with a strategy by tomorrow. And maybe call the lawyer.

Raj would have to testify in court. She wasn't sure how to spin that for the folks back home.

Enough. Time for sleep. Two beers and she was ready to pass out. Raj was already passed out. She broke her rule of no sleepovers when Raj was there and Alani spent the night. She felt so safe in his arms. It had been too long. Teresa slept with Raj, as she had done almost every night since his arrival.

Chapter 11

Raj and Teresa slept late the next morning. K.O. let Alani sleep but she was trained to wake up at nearly the same time. It was a curse, but it allowed her some alone-time. Coffee in hand, seated in the recliner watching her beautiful mountains, she almost felt normal. The phone rang. Crap. It had been repaired. Probably Maureen and she wasn't ready for that. It was three hours later in Seattle, so Maureen had been raring to go for hours.

K.O. sighed and answered. Not Maureen. Detective Keahi with an update. K.O. listened with a grunt of acknowledgement or surprise once in a while. Bottom line, Raj would have to testify, but Goto was in the hospital in stable condition. At the snail's pace of the court system, the trial would be months away at the earliest.

Alani wandered out of the bedroom headed to the coffee pot. "Morning."

"Morning." K.O. had just hung up. She caught him up quickly. Raj might not wake up for hours, but she decided to get the Maureen phone call part one, out of the way. She had already decided not to mention the murder or Raj's driving issues.

K.O. picked up her coffee mug and got a refill. "Gonna need all my strength for this," she told Alani. Alani had met her family since they had been an on-again off-again couple for years. They had broken up over K.O. turning him in about a murder a few years ago. It had been a mess, but many nights of long conversations and a 'time out' had resulted in the decision to stay together. Despite their differing heritage, culture and jobs, they could not deny their connectedness and need for each other. Alani was quite familiar with Maureen's personality, but he and her husband Joe got along well and surfed together when they visited.

"Good luck. Remember, less is more."

She did know. She only had to say one sentence, any sentence, and Maureen would carry the rest of the conversation for as long as K.O.'d let her. Today, she planned to stick to the facts and spend the rest of the time soothing the mama lion.

Caller I.D. was not her friend. The second Maureen picked up, she was already talking.

"I tried to call you and call you! All the phone lines were down and I just watched the news and worried." Maureen ran on in this vein. "I want to talk to Raj."

Finally a break. "He's sleeping, but I wanted to let you know he's fine. The waves have been really good *(an exaggeration)* and Raj has surfed better than projected so he's actually qualified to compete this weekend."

"What?" A moment of silence. "I can't possibly make it there in time to see him!"

That had not occurred to K.O. "No, it's fine. No worries. They video tape the whole contest and I'll make sure you don't miss a thing." Some sputtering. "I'll call you every night after and let you know how the day went, okay? I'll even have him talk to you. He can give you the blow by blow." Poor choice of words.

"Okay. Are you sure he's not up yet?"

"Let me check." K.O. opened her bedroom door. Raj's door was closed. "No, he's still asleep. We had a full day yesterday with the heats in the morning and then you know the crazy traffic."

K.O. completely omitted that she wasn't even there—she'd been in court. And the ensuing car chase. Could you call it a chase if one vehicle is a Papaya with four wheels that might possibly go as fast as a thrown papaya? Um, and toss in Raj running over someone who was trying to kill him. Nope, she'd leave it at 'a full day.'

K.O. could tell Maureen was split between fear for her 'baby' and pride at his success. K.O. understood a little: when she hadn't known where Raj was yesterday; when she'd found evidence of another crime at the team sponsor house and then wondered what would have happened if Goto had made it to Raj with the tire iron before Raj's lack of skill with manual transmissions hadn't come into play. Jeez, now she was sounding like Maureen. Well, they *were* sisters.

K.O. got off the phone with a promise that Raj would call today. She remembered the contest

180

was supposed to start today, if the waves cooperated. Shouldn't Jet have called by now? Anybody with an update?

She came out of the bedroom as Raj shot out of his. "Gotta get going. I surf today!"

His good night's sleep cured him, at least temporarily. K.O. decided not to tell him what Keahi had told her. Goto had confessed in the hospital and had a lot to say. However, she wanted Raj only to think about surfing. Maybe she'd tell him after his heat today.

Christmas was creeping toward them and she had done nothing. On the plus side, she had postponed a horrible confrontation with Maureen and that filled her with relief. She and Raj discussed his surf day as he ate a quick breakfast.

"You coming?" she asked Alani who remained in the recliner.

"Can't today. Another order. I do want to see the little rajah surf though. Maybe tomorrow." He referred to Raj's nickname from babyhood. He was the chubbiest baby and was very calm and still for an infant. When he learned to sit up, he would sit, rolls of fat pooched over his diaper, calmly observing his world. They started calling him Little Rajah, but when he got older, it became Raj as in king-of-the-surf. For his age, he was an amazing talent. K.O. felt fierce pride at his success at only fifteen.

No wonder a surf company snatched him up. Too bad BBB was run by weasels, she thought. But today would be different. She thought they all knew he wouldn't even come in the top five, but to be listed at all! To be up on the boards with the big guys, Kelly Slater, Rob Machado, Eddie Aikau.

"Come on, let's go," she called to cover her emotion. She kissed Alani good-bye and Raj bro-hugged him.

On the drive north, she distracted him by recounting her phone call with his mom. She made it as light-hearted and humorous as possible.

"She wanted to fly right out to be here! She's amazing," K.O. finished.

"I think it's better she not. I'm nervous enough."

"Look at the sky. It's gorgeous."

"It's not the sky," Raj began, "It's the waves," they finished together.

"Okay, I drop you here and park. Check your line up and I find you." K.O. pulled up right in front of the Billabong Pipe Masters banner.

She knew if the waves were good, there might be eight hours of heats. A surfer could surf five or six heats, maybe more. Exhausting and dangerous by the end. She didn't know if Raj had that kind of stamina. *Odds were,* she mused as she searched for a parking spot, *he wouldn't last past today. Day one. But that's okay. Gotta start somewhere.*

Traffic was crazy as usual, crawling along bumper to bumper. The Pipe Masters was the last contest in the Triple Crown and, with the storms of the past week keeping everyone indoors, and the rumors now flying about BBB and Robert Goto, this was a show not to be missed.

Saturday. She took a chance and parked at Sunset Beach Elementary. She added her official blue bubble. Not kosher, but she didn't want to miss Raj. He needed her there.

She trotted across the street, wending her way through masses of enthusiastic surfers and fans. A dense row of photographers lined the beach. Crowds of people made it impossible for her to find Raj. She went to the boards and asked what color jersey and what heat. The 'dude' with the clipboard looked askance.

"I'm his Auntie." That's all she needed to say. Family first, especially in the islands. *Ohana* is everything, whether by blood or love.

"Blue today. He's up in two heats."

"Mahalo." Two heats gave her a little while to find him, but first she'd check the surf, like he'd taught her.

"Holy cow," she muttered. The beach had shifted again from the storm surge, different from the way the previous storm had left it. The ridge was high and steep. The waves looked like buildings, towering over the sand even at this distance.

Jet-skis patrolled the edges of the curls and she noted the Beach Rescue teams on high alert. Lines of boats loaded with staff and more photographers bobbed about, unconcerned with the crush of waves, only with getting *the* shot. Already she was uncomfortable with Raj going out there. Knowing him, he was too. It looked bigger than anything he'd surfed before. She also knew he'd never bow out.

She wouldn't have either. That family stubborn streak made for unwise choices at times.

*   *   *   *

This time when Raj checked in, he was treated like a big deal. Well, compared to the last few times. Realistically, he knew he would be eliminated fairly early. The talent amassed here was incredible and more than a little daunting. Add to that the size of the waves and his blood ran pretty cold.

Kahana, Dylan and his 'groupies' had been watching for him. He was grateful since now, although he was offered a board, he hesitated to take one. He wanted Dylan's. Da Lucky Board.

They also wore bright pink tee shirts with his name written in Sharpie, proclaiming them his 'team.' Felt good.

Up until now, he hadn't allowed himself to think about all the competition. Hundreds of athletes. Most were eliminated in the early rounds. Three-man heats, then two-man heats. Then the quarterfinals and the semi-finals where the heats were fewer and competition fiercer.

He told Kahana he needed to focus. He thanked Dylan for the board, but his mind was in the water. He stretched and waxed his board watching the heats before his. The ocean was rough. A couple guys just fell off the wave when it got too steep too fast. He saw he'd need to really stomp the tail of his board, keep the fin in the water and stay low.

His heat was called. Round One. If he scored high enough, he could make it to Round Two. Felt weird with only three guys on the waves. All eyes on him pretty much. He didn't know the other two, except by name. They had made it the same as he had, but anything could happen. The paddle out had been intimidating. Jet skis, rescue guys, a helicopter, boats behind the line, and pushing through massive waves to get outside. His stomach quivered. "Just breathe," he heard in his head. He concentrated. Let the first swell build and pass. One of the others took it. Hard to see but looked like a decent ride. At least he didn't fall off.

Raj reoriented himself on the wave. The swell built under him and he was out far enough he could correct. He barely needed to paddle before the wave picked him up. It happened so fast he instantly understood how those guys fell off. One second he was in the sea, the next he felt he was dangling above it. The wave was so long he knew he could do a couple things to boost his score. The wedgie-peaky wave was perfect for a backside air reverse. He inverted his board underneath him, tail to the top, then swung his arms up to get some height and kept the board under him. He stomped the tail on the lip of the wave like he'd told himself to, over the white wash and avoided landing in the flats. That would have been interesting, since from way up here, the flats looked a mile away.

Raj felt the barrel looming behind him and risked a glance. He took it and was inside. It raced to consume him and instead of a nice clean exit, all he saw was foam. He crouched and allowed the

185

pipe to roll him a bit, up and down inside. Again, he felt something in there with him. He knew it was Tiger shark, but all he could think about was staying on his stick. He had to get out past the foam before the barrel collapsed.

He aimed for the center of the foam and shot out, arms up, mid-wave. He rode down and up, carving an S in the side of the wave. He imagined he heard the crowds cheering, but really he heard nothing, not even his pounding heart, except the crush of the sea. He hit the flats and was about to go over the backside when he heard the horn. Time. Tiger shark had disappeared.

As he rode a little wobbler in, he enjoyed his view of the cheering crowd. People standing, seated, jumping up and down. He knew they weren't his fans, but fans of the sport. He took his time. Who knew if he'd have this moment again?

*   *   *   *

K.O. managed to get a place standing on the rise. Most folks were pretty nice about sharing. She mentioned her nephew was out there, and the masses parted for her. *Ohana.*

She watched him study the water while he waxed his board. Where did he get that board? She hadn't seen hide nor hair of Jet. Whatever. She was going to break Raj's contract with BBB if it was the last thing she did.

He looked small and thin, but whip strong. Young. She stood far from where he readied himself, but she had a good view of his shock of sun-bleached dark hair and firm jaw.

A horn. Three jerseys paddled out—only one blue. With only three surfers to watch, it was easy to pick out Raj from her years of watching him. When they waited behind the line, she could see nothing while the wave built.

The first guy took off. Big wave. Scary wave. He stayed on, which was more than some had. She empathized with them—disappointing after making it this far. At least they weren't hurt. No one had died this year. Why did she think that? Re-focus on Raj.

A long wave built and Raj adjusted his board. She thought he was going to let it pass, but it swept him up like a giant hand. She stopped breathing. He stayed back on his board. The drop was forever and the swell continued to build behind him. Then he did a flippy-doodle. She couldn't believe it. He actually turned his board around on the wave—he and his board were airborne for a moment, then he threw his arms in the air before being swept into a long tube of water. Her heart stayed in her mouth until he erupted out of the foam and slid toward the beach, doing a cocky little roller-coaster thing he'd done since he'd first started surfing. He continued on until the horn.

She remembered to breathe. She looked for the third surfer, but he'd attempted the same wave and had fallen off. He was fine and paddled to catch a small foamy wave into the beach.

K.O. raced to where Raj'd get out of the water, but she underestimated his new-found popularity. He was mobbed. She smiled. She'd catch up with him later and went to the judge's stand to wait.

She was finally close enough to hear the announcers. "That was newcomer, Raj Dela Cruz from Washington state, folks. He must be stoked on that last transaction. He was drawing a line fitting in the barrel. A nice ride from this beginner. I think we're going to see more of this young man."

K.O.'s heart swelled with pride and love. She definitely would have something to tell her sister tonight. She didn't know how this all worked, but given the other two riders in Raj's heat, she was sure he'd make it to Round Two tomorrow. He'd be high as a kite and there'd be no peeling him off the ceiling.

Maybe she'd invite Alani to dinner and they'd all have *that* conversation about Robert Goto and what he'd been up to. Raj deserved to know what happened, and that none of this was his fault.

Chapter 12

K.O. spent the rest of the day following Raj around while he checked stats and met his new fans. A group of pink-clad teens obviously knew him, particularly a pretty local girl with long brown hair and flashing dark eyes who was never far away.

Finally Raj allowed that they could leave. K.O. had managed to call Alani on the now repaired pay phone, again vowing to look into getting herself a cell phone. He agreed to meet at her place for dinner.

The ride down from the North Shore was filled with Raj's chatter about his ride. He mentioned the shark. Twice.

K.O. blanched but hid it. What if Maureen found out about that? What if he'd been injured or worse? She regathered her calm.

"So, you saw it twice or there were two sharks?" K.O. asked as they pulled into her parking space.

"It was two different days and I didn't ask for I.D."

"Did anybody else say anything? Did you tell anyone?"

"No. I forgot by the time I got out of the water. I know, sounds weird, but so much going on, yeah?"

K.O. unlocked the front door. "I know."

"Besides, I dunno, was like it was surfing, too. I think I touched it."

K.O. stopped, startled.

"Touched what?" Alani asked, coming from the living room.

"Oh, nothing. Only a tiger shark in the waves with him."

"No kidding, little man. Tell me." Alani guided Raj to the comfy recliners while K.O. pulled out pasta and jarred sauce to prep dinner.

Raj told Alani what he'd already said to K.O. on the drive.

"Close your eyes," Alani said. "Think what you were doing and what happened."

"Okay, but I only really saw a shadow the first time. The next time, I had my hand out in the barrel, you know like you do." Alani nodded. He was a surfer, too. "And, it was firm, you know? I was startled. It was rougher than the wave and darker, but it was so fast, I don't know. Thought it was one dolphin. Maybe I didn't believe it for real. Not 'til I saw it again. Today for shua, was one shark!"

"You never saw it while you were waiting outside?" Alani referred to when the surfers straddle their boards beyond the break waiting for the set.

"No. I nevah even t'ink about it. I was so nervous. And everything so big and moving so fast."

"Lemme think." Alani closed his eyes and stayed that way.

Raj tiptoed into the kitchen where K.O. slathered garlic butter on sourdough. "What's going on? What he doing?"

"You know he's Hawai'ian, right?" Raj rolled his eyes in the classic 'duh' teenager response. "He's a kahuna. He's getting in touch with his ancestors to ask about manō. Shark."

"What's he asking?"

"I have a guess, but he's doing all the work, so I'm going to let him tell you."

"Auntie!"

"Set the table. He's far away right now, but try not to drop anything. Shhh."

By the time K.O. and Raj had finished getting dinner ready, Alani was back with them.

"Alani, what did you find out?" Raj asked.

"Manō is your *aumakua*. That's why he surfed with you."

"What's that again?" Raj had spent enough time in the islands to have heard most of the cultural lore, but he had the attention span of a normal kid.

"*Aumakua* is your animal spirit. He was there to protect you. But you also have responsibilities to your *aumakua*. Your Auntie knows."

"I do? I have an *aumakua*?" K.O. was startled. "Can *haoles* have them? I thought only Hawai'ians have them."

191

"Spirit protectors are in every culture, but since you live here, yours is here, too."

"How did I get an *aumakua*? And how do you know it and I don't?"

"Yours is the 'elepaio. The little bird."

"I would not have guessed that. I would have thought a cat or something." K.O. passed around the pasta bowl. "Dish up while it's hot."

"The two are connected. Remember I said that Raj has responsibilities too, in exchange for the protection manō gave him and will continue to give him?"

"Yes, I remember." Raj nodded too, mouth full of garlic bread.

"You began by saving 'elepaio. Remember that time when Teresa brought the bird into the house and you rescued it?"

"Yes, it was only scared. Teresa was actually very gentle, considering how small it was."

"That act was part of your agreement. You helped it, and it will help you."

"How is a little bird going to help me?"

"That remains to be seen."

"Hey, how did you even know about that? I didn't tell you."

"It did right now."

"Wow, this is so weird!" Raj exclaimed. "Pass the salad, please. What about me? How am I supposed to help a shark? That thing was twice my size if it was an inch. It could have taken a big chunk out of me, but it didn't. I've never saved a shark before."

"Your responsibilities may lie in the future. But you must never harm a shark, and you will be safe in the water from them."

"All sharks or just tigers?"

"Manō is a family, but I wouldn't press my luck if you know what I mean." Alani managed to get in a couple bites while Raj considered this.

"Okay," K.O. said, "am I supposed to be related to all birds now or only 'elepaio?"

"You are not related, but you have a relationship. Just because you don't understand it, don't discount it."

They ate in silence for a few minutes. Raj finally nodded. "Cool. I get it."

Alani smiled.

K.O. jumped in. "Oh, I have a lot to tell you both about Robert Goto. I know you have a big day ahead tomorrow, Raj, but I want to catch you up. Detective Keahi called me but I thought it was better to let you concentrate on your day today."

"Oh, shoots, yeah. What happened?"

"I'll try and keep it short since I promised your mom you'd call and let her know how your day went."

Raj made a face K.O. couldn't decode. Pride? Love? The slight slump of shoulders of the world-weary teen could mean a lot of things.

"It started because Jet wanted to take his company public. Well, I guess it started before that. Let me back up. Bad Boyz Beach is a little company, but Jet wanted it to be bigger. So, he got surfers like Aliki, and you Raj, but he also needed more experienced help. He tried to do things the right way, but then he started to cut corners. He was basically a surfer with a good idea. He needed a financial guy because he knew nothing about that end of the business. That's where Robert Goto came in."

"The house chaperone?" Raj asked.

"Yes. He had a history of creative accounting, as it were, that made companies leery of hiring him. Jet didn't have a lot of money, but he needed the expertise Goto could bring. Everyone at BBB had to do double duty, like Jet did the hiring and PR, handled the merchandising, etc., and Goto was the house chaperone, did the books and filed official papers. What nobody knew was that Goto had a gambling problem. He thought being inside a surf company would give him an edge and when he bet, he bet big. He lost big on the surf contests. He owed a lot of money to some not very nice people." Both Alani and Raj were rapt at attention.

"They bet on surfing?" Raj asked.

"People will bet on anything but yes, it's big business and not illegal. However, the people Goto bet through were hard core and they weren't through legal channels. He couldn't pay it back and started embezzling out of BBB to cover. That might have worked if he'd had more time. But Jet wanted to go public fast. He wanted the promotion and wins from the Reef Hawai'ian Pro, the O'Neill World Cup and the Billabong Pipe Masters to induce his investment bank into making the IPO." At Raj's blank look K.O. added, "Initial Public Offering. Jet, as you know, could be pretty aggressive and Aliki started strong-arming people to move the project forward. Jet wanted Goto to get all the paperwork ready for the bankers. Once the bankers got it, Goto knew it wouldn't pass muster or get the company onto the New York Stock Exchange. He tried to cook the books, but again, he didn't have enough time. He knew the SEC would find out at some point. Meanwhile, he'd have his legs broken or worse when he couldn't pay his own debts."

"Wow. But why kill Eldon? And try for me? What did I do?"

"It was a case of wrong place, wrong time for Eldon. Turns out Eldon is—was studying to be a CPA and was a Math major at UH. Eldon found his stash of double books and knew what he was looking at. Eldon had to go. We came into the house that same day, so Goto stuffed him under the bed and hid in the closet. He was going to move him later, but I found the body and everything changed fast."

"So, you were both in the room with a murderer and the body of the victim?" Alani asked.

"Yup. I'm not sure what would have happened if he'd jumped out of the closet and started clubbing away." K.O. sipped her wine to cover her anxiety. She felt she could have protected herself, but protect Raj, too? That wouldn't have turned out so well.

Raj picked at a fingernail. "So, when I came back during the storm, he knew I'd seen him, that he'd been there, and that he was the one who killed Eldon. That's why I had to go. That was so scary."

195

"I don't understand how Goto knew you knew," Alani said.

"Shoes!" both Raj and K.O. said.

Alani's eyebrows went up. Raj explained about the team shoes. K.O. nodded, shivering again at how close a call they'd both had, seeing the neon shoes, with feet in them, in the closet.

Raj started to shake and K.O. went over to comfort him. "It's okay. You got away and now he's behind bars."

"He'll have to testify, right?" Alani rose and squeezed Raj's shoulder.

"Probably not if Goto sticks to his story. He's confessed and there won't be a trial unless he recants. I think the Papaya incident will be dropped."

"What Papaya incident?" Alani asked.

K.O. and Raj looked guilty. "I guess I forgot to mention that," K.O. said.

"Little bit." Alani sat back down.

Sweat beaded Raj's upper lip. "To get away from Goto, I took the Papaya and ended up at the SatCom site. I was trapped and he was coming to get me with a tire iron and I didn't know it was in gear and I sort of . . . accidentally ran him over."

K.O. burst out laughing. "I know, I know, it's wrong. But it's kind of funny. He was a bad person. He's not dead, so it's funny."

Raj smiled a little, too, but his eyes never left Alani's face.

A moment of heavy silence. "You didn't dent my car, though, right?"

Chapter 13

As they cleaned up dinner Raj asked, "So, what about Aliki? He didn't kill Eldon, but why did he miss his heat?"

K.O. rinsed dishes and loaded them in the dishwasher. "He wasn't doing well surfing and that upset him. He was really mad that a little pipsqueak like you was ahead of him. He got a little blitzed the night before, apparently. He drank too much and woke up with a screaming hangover and in a terrible mood. He made the strategy meeting at the hotel, but only after Myles Freeh cornered him about dropping in. If he hadn't been so hungover it would have been fine, you know, because you can't see over the wave sometimes." K.O. said this as if she knew what she was talking about. Raj and Alani nodded in understanding. "Anyway, he was an ass and Myles wasn't going to put up with it. That's what we saw on the way in to the hotel. After the meeting, he passed out in one of the other surfer's rooms and missed his heat."

"Did they find out what happened to my board?" Raj misinterpreted her look and rushed on,

"I know it's not important to the case, but I wondered."

"I know it's important to you. It's important to me, too. I asked Keahi if he knew. He told me that when they interrogated Aliki, he told them all about you and he doesn't remember specifically breaking your board, but he remembers having it the night before and messing with it. He knows how important a board is."

"I knew was him! But, did Goto use it to kill Eldon? That would be so horrible. I wanted to keep my board anyway, but . . ."

"No worries there. I'm sorry I didn't tell you before, your board wasn't the murder weapon."

"I knew it was the tire iron!"

"No, not that either. I thought it was a little weird he'd have a tire iron in the bedroom, but stranger things have happened."

"Well, what then?" Raj asked.

"Was a poi pounder."

"What's a poi pounder?"

K.O. looked at Alani. "You take this one."

"It's a heavy piece of lava carved into a sort of pyramid shape with a heavy base contoured up to a narrow top you can hold. Got like a little bulge at the top so your hand doesn't slip." He held his hands about six inches apart. "About this big, maybe, but heavy. Good weapon and easy to grab. Used to mash taro root into poi."

K.O. jumped back in. "You know the house had all this Hawai'ian stuff for decoration?" Raj nodded. "Well, it had a poi pounder, too. I remember seeing it sitting on its base, but I didn't think about it."

"So glad it's not my board."

"Goto washed it off after we left, but Jeanine, she takes everything. Everything even if she doesn't know it's evidence. I can learn a lot from her if I'm gonna make detective."

"You going for detective now?" Alani asked.

"Some day."

"You just made sergeant."

"They're the same rank but I won't get to be a sergeant if I go to CID."

"CID?" Raj asked.

"Criminal Investigation Division. I would investigate crimes like this among other things."

"Why would you *want* to?" Raj shuddered.

"To help people like you," K.O. answered.

Raj shook his head and then went to call his mom. Alani and K.O. held hands on the loveseat watching the ribbon falls trickle down the emerald mountains.

"You coming tomorrow, right? To watch Raj surf?" K.O. asked. "It's probably his last day. I was surprised he made it."

"I wouldn't miss it. Maybe manō helped him surf those days."

"You really believe that?"

"K.O., we've been through this before. My heritage is part of me. It's not something I can separate and pick and choose." He rubbed a gentle circle on her clasped hand with his thumb. "I've seen so many things I can't explain any other way."

"That shark, not coincidence? I mean, they're everywhere."

"Believe what you like. But maybe there's a way to make it a little less coincidental for you."

"How?"

"You'll have to wait and see."

"Alani, no way."

"I know patience isn't your strong suit. Take a page from your other *aumakua's* book." He nodded to Teresa, sleeping coiled in a recliner. "She waits and waits and finally, she gets what she wants. Usually."

"Like a bird. Until I took it away from her."

"Did you ever think maybe she was bringing it to you? You said she could have hurt or killed it, and didn't. Further, she let you take it from her. Most cats will keep their prey, not hand it over."

"I guess." She started to say more, but Alani forestalled it by kissing her. They broke apart when Raj returned from his call. All was well. The settled in to watch *"Blue Juice,"* another surf movie.

*   *   *   *

Sunday dawned spectacularly, and Raj was up with the sun. His heat was not until later, but he was excited. He knew it was probably his last day. He would be eliminated, but that was okay. It was a joy to be here, to experience all of this. It would make him ready for next year. And there *would* be a next year.

He was about to pound on his Auntie's bedroom door when she staggered out, aimed directly for the coffee pot. He'd learned at an early age how to make coffee. He smiled remembering years ago when he'd had to drag a chair to reach the counter. Those first few batches were probably awful, but she never said. That was what was so good about her. She didn't nag like his mom. He didn't mind the nagging so much; he knew his mom loved him, but sometimes, it was nice for someone not to get all *huhu* at you. *Even when you deserved it.*

He didn't want to think about Robert Goto and the Papaya, how close to being hurt or worse he'd really come, but those thoughts wouldn't be ignored. His heart filled when he thought about his Auntie. He knew she would die to protect him. He'd seen something in her face when she'd come running to him at the SatCom site. He wouldn't want to be a criminal, that's for sure.

"Auntie, you ready?" Raj said, laughing, because clearly she was not. Her red hair stuck out in tufts and her face showed the strain and wear of the last few days. Uncharacteristically, he crossed to her and gave her a tight hug.

"You da bes'," he mumbled into her hair. He was almost as tall as she. That surprised him a little. He was used to her being so big, but he would be taller and stronger than her by next visit. "Thank you fo' everyt'ing you do fo' me."

She hugged him. Her hands were strong on his back and again he thought of how she'd fought to protect him.

"I gon' win today, Auntie!" He swung her around toward the coffee pot.

"Yeah?" was all she managed.

"No ways, Auntie! But I feel so good right now. Dis da beginning fo' me! I goin' do my bes', but those guys, *no ka oi*, man! They numbah one, but I feel like I won. I going ask my *aumakua* fo' help today."

"You sure you want to do that?" K.O. added creamer and sweetener to her Kona coffee.

"Why not? He's been there anyway, might as well make one reques'!" Raj laughed again. He couldn't help it. "Come on, let's go. My last day as an official entrant. I got fans, brah!" He ran to his room to get ready.

K.O. told him on the drive up that Alani would meet them there. He got more focused the closer they got.

"I drop you and park, okay?"

He nodded. He felt hyperaware. This was the last time he would be here, in this place, in these circumstances. He wanted to remember it. He really looked at the Billabong sign, the welcome arch, the list of those who died surfing here. All were sobering in different ways. He took off his rubber slippers and felt the chill of the sand before the sun hit it. The scratch of ironwood needles and shards of wood. The smell of clean air and wild ocean along with the barbeques starting their long day of cranking out meat for plate lunches. Not too many folks here yet. The sun was low in the east. Day Two, Round Two. He watched the buzz of the surfers; a lot of them in the competition. Still hope. He tried to guess who would make it to the quarter finals. Myles Freeh for sure. Tai Phillips. Eldon probably would have. That made him sad. Eldon's name wouldn't even go up on the losses board, because he didn't die doing what he loved: surfing. He was murdered by a selfish criminal. Raj's resolve hardened. He wouldn't win, he knew that. He wasn't giving up, but he simply didn't have the skills at this level of competition. But he would someday. He promised himself that. And his *aumakua.*

He studied the waves. "You out there?" he asked his *aumakua.*

"Hey!" Kahana jumped out of nowhere. "You did so good yesterday! We're rooting for you again!" She wore her pink shirt with the Sharpie slogan.

Startled, Raj's heart raced a bit. "Hey. Thanks. Dylan bring da lucky board?"

"Fo' shua! Dylan!" She turned and yelled across the sand, further scattering Raj's focus.

She meant well, but he would have to get away from her to concentrate. Didn't she say she surfed for the women's team? How much did she actually surf? He didn't know any girl surfers, not serious ones anyway. His sister Justine only surfed for fun, and that was almost never now. She would graduate high school this year and was looking at colleges. Not college in Hawaii, though. *Focus, focus.* His mind was drifting.

Dylan sauntered up with the board. His energy was much more relaxed. "Hey, brah." They hand slapped. "We goin' watch for you. When's your heat?"

203

Good question. "I'd better go check in."
And *think*. "Mahalo, brah. I see you later. You too,
Kahana." Before he could escape, she kissed his
cheek.

"For luck!" she said as she bounced off.

"Whoa, she make me so tired," Dylan said.

"You read my mind," Raj agreed. They both
laughed watching her go down the beach, greeting
everyone with a hug and a smile. "She's a good
person."

"I think so too," Dylan said. "Even if not, I
stuck wit' her." He trundled off in the direction
Kahana had gone, toward a group of pink tee shirts.

Raj headed over to check the standings and
today's roster. During those few minutes with
Kahana and Dylan the sun had risen above the trees
and once again the strip of beach glowed like light
brown sugar.

He loved seeing his name written there. His
wave yesterday gave him 13.83. A decent score.
Far away from some like Myles Freeh with a 15.80,
but not like poor Aaron Hill with 1.23.

From yesterday's twelve three-man heats it
went down to twelve two-man heats today. He was
up against someone he didn't know, but who had
won his heat yesterday.

He was in heat six and who knew what the
weather would be like by then. Yesterday he'd
been earlier, so watching the waves made him feel,
right or wrong, that he could 'plan.' But you could
never really plan. Each set was different, and each
wave in the set could change. That's what made it
so exciting and challenging.

Auntie joined him standing on the ridge of sand, watching the water. The announcers were calling the heats and the crowd had gathered rapidly. The water filled with craft, both safety and observational, and he heard the now-familiar flap-flap of the helicopter as it began its circular pattern of filming it all. The contest day began.

"I gotta go Auntie. I'm sorry. I have to concentrate," Raj apologized.

"No worries. Alani will be here soon. I won't be bored. Now that I understand this better, it's more interesting."

"And now that no one's trying to kill us, more relaxing, yeah Auntie?"

"Fo' shua." Auntie gave him a high five and took her turtle beach bag, her satellite dish-sized sun hat and headed to 'her' tree. It comforted him to know she was always near if he needed her.

Raj stayed close enough to the stand to hear the commentary. The waves were not as high as before the storm, but were fast-running walls.

Eric Lee, a BBB surfer, was up in this heat. The morning air had a chill, but the water looked great.

The play by play announcer kicked in. "Eric Lee has experience out here, but he's never made it very far. He's got to read that wave beautifully in order to stay with it."

Raj watched Lee do just that. Lee knew instinctively where to be on the wave. The commentator continued, "Okay, a couple of solid moves to get started. Putting a ton of rail in the water—looks really spicy. And he's out."

Lee had a great ride from what Raj could tell. He thought Lee felt so too, since he rolled right in to the foam and then fell sideways off the board, wearing a big smile.

The next couple heats were similar, the waves even but big. Nice barrels and no accidents. Raj tried to match his inner commentary to what he saw and heard. It would help him on his own ride later. His stomach growled. Time had flown and it was noon, the straight up sun confirming time to eat. He went to the participants' tent and scrounged. Mostly snacks, but a Hawai'ian Sun Passion-Orange-Guava—POG—hit the spot. He had a package of nuts for some protein, but what he really wanted was a plate lunch. He grabbed some more nuts and another drink and returned to his viewing post.

Along with the afternoon came a shift in the water. Less smooth, more unpredictable, each set was different from the last. That's what he'd been worried about.

Heat five. He stretched. Waxed his board. Buddy Soarez, a Vans surfer from Hawai'i grabbed a wave. The commentator began. "This wall is just standing up. Soarez looks good going in. He sailed through the Reef and World Cup, so this could be a real winner here, folks. Oh, clean rap right there—so stylish. Full rail carve into the pocket! He's looking to improve and he just might do it!"

Raj agreed. Soarez won his heat. The other surfer chose a wave that was more muddled and choppy and he was unable to really show what he

206

needed. Raj knew it was as important to choose the right wave as it was to choose what to do *on* that wave. The wave statistics were listed as well as the surfers' scores. The total number of waves surfed and then each wave was rated and used to compile the surfers' score. Yesterday when Raj had surfed, a total of 160 waves were counted in 12 heats. Of those waves, only 71 waves were used for tabulation. They were rated Excellent, Good, Regular, or Poor and affected the overall score. Yesterday, there were 15 Excellent, 17 Good, 15 Regular and 23 Poor. How that was tabulated with all the numbers calculated was like throwing it all in a big blender to Raj.

Statistics were never Raj's strong suit and he only started geometry this year in tenth grade. He was not having fun with that. He knew these numbers were important to his success, so he added that to the ever-growing mental list of things to do.

Raj's heat. He was on. "Just breathe," he told himself. He stepped into the water, toes curling at the chill and paddled out.

Only one other surfer. They eyed each other, but separated once outside. The lull between sets. Surfers who are friendly use that time to talk story, but not during competition. The sat astride their boards, each lost in concentration.

The familiar pull of a swell building. Raj glanced behind him. It felt good. Should he go? He hesitated a moment and it was decided for him. He missed it. The other surfer took it. Hard to tell how the ride was going from the back side, but Raj saw the board pop straight up and the surfer climbed on the lip of the wave before grabbing the board with his hands and dropping out of sight. Fantastic. Raj had not learned how to do that successfully and regularly. You only had a second to look at where you needed to go before you needed to be there. Raj's timing was not reliable and he often fell off before he could get the proper grip and balance.

His heart sank. Although he had expected to lose this heat, he didn't expect it to happen so fast. The next wave built. Focus. Pay attention. He glanced behind him to check his distance. Perfect. But he saw something else that made his heart squeeze. He knew exactly what that shadow in the wave was. No matter what Alani told him, he did not want to be sitting in the water with that monster. He paddled like crazy and hit the wall, climbing fast on the root of the wave. A nice flutter into a back hand snap and finish. The wave was long. He was able to add a backdoor barrel slot-through before he ran out of wave. Nice. However, no air for him, no real chances. He didn't make "A," the local term for making an ass of yourself, but the wave was good and he wasn't able to make more use of it. It felt that way at any rate. It wasn't a super high killer wave, or choppy or risky. His 'good' wave would lower his score. Whatever way he looked back at his ride, either the shark had told him to take that wave, or he was scared to stay in the water with it, the choice was made. It was done now. The horn. He paddled in toward a sea of pink tee shirts, his cheering Auntie and Alani, and what? His mother screaming her brains out, next to his dad and a smiling—for once—Justine.

*   *   *   *

Alani joined K.O. on the sand, adding a nice beach mat and a basket of snacks to the site.

"Where is he?" he asked once they'd established territory.

"There. He seems nervous." K.O. pointed out where Raj stood with his board, shoulders tight in concentration as he assessed the waves.

"Who's in his heat?"

"I don't know the guy. Not famous, but solid from what I heard. I know Raj thinks he's ready to lose this one, but he's not. Not really."

"You never are." Alani popped the top on a Pepsi. He'd brought Diet for K.O. knowing her weakness for it. He offered her a can.

"Thanks. The surf looks rougher than yesterday."

"It is. Yesterday was smooth, plus, the water's different in the morning. His heat's in two more. Gonna be hotter and the waves will change from now, too."

"How do you prepare for that?"

"Surf. All the time. In all conditions. In as many different places as you can. He's good you know."

"I know."

"No, I mean really good. Pro good. This year will be important for him. If the family's

209

willing to support him, he needs to go to J Bay, to Mavericks, everywhere he can get in."

"He's not going to have a sponsor. BBB is going under, and even if it weren't, I'd never let him stay with them."

"I know. But I have a buddy at Rip Curl and I told him about Raj."

"Isn't that an Australian company?"

"Yes."

"He won't have to move to Australia or anything? Mau would never go for that."

Alani laughed. "No. They have surfers from all over. But he will travel a lot. He has to be sure that's what he wants."

"I think he's up." K.O. stood and moved down the beach for a better look. A screech and she was encircled by at least two pairs of arms. After the massive hug she pulled back to see who it was. Her sister Maureen and niece Justine. Brother-in-law Joe stood back waiting his turn.

"Oh, my God? What are you guys—how did you get—" K.O. couldn't finish a sentence. Her brain couldn't quite wrap itself around Mau in Seattle yesterday and Mau on the North Shore now.

"Red eye!" Maureen exclaimed. "Once I heard his voice last night, I couldn't miss it. His one chance maybe. I've never seen him surf at this level so I got over my worry and called in 'family emergency' at work. Joe had a family emergency too." Maureen was ecstatic. Even mellow Joe was beaming and shifting his feet in the sand. "So last night we got on the first plane out and came straight here!"

"Where's Raj?" Justine asked.

"Oh, wow. They called his heat and I came down here. I think he's paddled out. Only two guys in the heat. Look!"

They strained to watch the first surfer grab a wave and effortlessly cling to the surface. "I don't think that's Raj," K.O. said.

"How can you tell?" Maureen asked.

"I been watching him surf for a while now. He's good, but he hesitates more, doesn't do that trick thing, that last one. At least, I've never seen him do it. Grab the board with his hands."

"Okay, so that means he's next," Justine said.

"Yeah. Hard to see over those waves. He's sitting outside now, waiting."

The crowd noise rose. "He must be going now; it's getting noisy," Maureen said. "I'm so nervous."

"I used to be, too, but we've been together now a while and he's okay." The week flashed by in K.O.'s head from the storm to the body to the shark. Shit. Lotta catching up to do. Maybe some editing, though.

"He's up!" Joe said. His tense body the only sign of nerves.

The announcer said, "This kid is one to watch. Up and comer from the Mainland, Raj Dela Cruz. You can tell his inexperience, but man, he is comfortable with the rhythm and pace of the wave. He never seems in a hurry. He doesn't make all the choices an experienced surfer might, but he's got raw talent and obvious determination. There's a floater into a tail release. Oh, he's not giving up yet. More water for him to use. And that's a backdoor barrel slot-through. Nicely done. I've never seen this kid *not* find a barrel to hit. Even if there's the tiniest pipe he squeezes in. Not a great wave, but he did a great job of it."

K.O. was again enveloped in a group crush. Alani got caught up in it, too.

"What happens now?" Justine asked.

"There's the horn. The heat's over. We wait and see what the scores are. The winner of each of these heats moves onto the next round."

"Well, he did great, didn't he?" Maureen asked.

"He did. He really did," K.O. answered.

"He'll make the next round for sure, right?" Justine asked.

K.O. was watching Alani. Both he and Joe had the experience. Alani shook his head.

Joe said, "I doubt it."

"What? Why?" Maureen looked mad.

"Mau, settle, don't shoot the messenger," K.O. hushed her sister.

"It doesn't matter so much that he rode well for him, it matters how well compared to the people in his heat usually."

"What you mean, usually?" Mau slipped into a little pidgin—when she was mad or had too many beers.

"Sometimes when earlier scores are really high, they can offset a later not so good score," Alani said. "But Raj doesn't have earlier high scores to fall back on."

"So it's over for him?" Justine looked about to cry.

"For this contest. But he knew that. We talked about it." K.O. rubbed her niece's back.

"He'll be bummed, it's natural," Joe said. "But he's going to go far. He's better now than I was at my best, and he's just starting."

Maureen looked at him. "Did you want to go pro?"

"Thought about it. But I really didn't have the talent. Only the love. Then I went to college and met this hottie, and well, surfing became a hobby."

Maureen leaned in and kissed her husband. "See how well that turned out." Joe wrapped her in his arms.

Alani had been watching the water. "He's coming up the beach!"

Maureen and Justine ran down to greet him trailed by K.O. and the men. K.O. had one glimpse of Raj's shocked face before he was smothered in family. As it should be.

After Raj recovered, his groupies got a shot at him. A ring of pink tees encircled by other fans reached to clap him on the back and a boy relieved him of the board. They herded him toward the judges' stand even as the air horn blew for the next heat.

The family caught up to him by the stand.

"Oh, my gosh," Raj said. I can't believe you guys are here! I just talked to you last night!"

"When I heard your voice and you told me about your ride yesterday, I knew I couldn't miss today," Maureen said.

"Me neither. Couldn't miss my boy," Joe said.

"I was already out of school for winter break, so I didn't care!" Justine added, but she looked proud, too.

"Did you see my ride?" Raj asked everyone. They all nodded. "Not so good?" he directed to his dad and Alani, the de facto surf experts.

"Your ride was good," Alani said.

"The wave was not that good," his dad said. "I know it's hard to tell sometimes when you on the back side waiting."

"I wasn't sure. Something *made* me take it." Raj looked uncertain.

"What do you mean, made you?" his mother asked.

Raj shuffled his feet in the sand. "A shark was in the waves with me. I got kinda scared."

"Oh, my God!" Justine shrieked. "I would so totally die if that happened to me."

"Your shark?" Alani asked.

Raj nodded as Joe asked, "What do you mean *your* shark?"

"The last few times I surfed, a big Tiger shark was out there with me."

"Why didn't you say anything?" his mother scolded. "Won't they postpone or cancel or something?"

"Maybe, but I didn't want that. I was scared, but I didn't feel in danger."

"How would you know?" Maureen sounded on the verge of hysteria. "This surfing thing is not worth your life!"

"Maureen," Alani put his hand on her arm. "It's okay. Nothing happened."

"But it might."

"A lot of t'ings *might* happen," said Joe. "You can't live your life worried about *might* alla time."

"Mom. By the time I saw the shark with me, I'd really already decided to take that wave. It made me firm up my choice. I took it and I gave it my best shot. I don't think I did better than the other guy in my heat, but I know I did the best I could. I'm going to keep going. Get more experience. The shark is not part of that."

"Well," Joe started.

"I think it might be," Alani said.

Joe looked at him. "What do you mean?"

"Manō is Raj's *aumakua.*"

"Oh, that," Joe said.

"What do you mean, 'oh that'?" Maureen was about to melt down.

"Manō my family *aumakua*. He get it from me," Joe said.

"I, I, you . . ." Maureen could only sputter.

Justine burst out laughing. "My mom can't talk! That's awesome!"

Maureen turned her glare onto her daughter. K.O. hugged her sister hard. "Let it go, sis. Let it go. It's going to be all right."

"Just breathe," Raj and K.O. said together.

"Scores out," Alani said.

They all turned. "Shoots," Raj said. 9.2 for Raj. His competitor got 9.8. Pretty close, but not good enough. He would not continue on.

"I knew was like that," Raj said. He sounded down, but not devastated.

"Raj, I think you're going to do well if you decide to continue on. If your parents let you," Alani said.

"Of course. We support him if he wants to do this," Joe said.

"I'll have to think about it," Maureen said.

A chorus of "Mom," "Mau," "Honey," rang out. Maureen looked a little sheepish. "Well, I will. I'm losing my baby this year. And I thought I'd have more time with this one." She put her arm around Raj.

"What are you talking about?" Joe asked.

"Justine. She's leaving us. Or don't you remember?" Maureen had some of her vinegar back.

"She's not dying. She's going to college. And you don't even know where she's going. She might go to UW and live at home!" Joe said.

"Over my dead body," Justine said.

K.O. laughed. "You guys. I love my family so much!"

"So much you live 3000 miles away," Maureen said.

"That's about right," K.O. answered.

"I totally get that. Can I go UH and live with you Auntie?" Justine asked.

"No!" everyone said.

"Hey, someone here for Raj," Alani said. K.O. thought it would be the pink posse headed by the pretty girl, but it was a tall, blonde haole in his thirties wearing a Rip Curl tee and jams.

"This is my friend Ryan Bauer from Rip Curl. He's here to talk to Raj for a minute, if that's okay?" Alani said by way of introduction.

Raj didn't wait for his family's permission. "Great! Let's go by the picnic tables." He led Rip Curl Ryan away before anyone had a chance to grill him.

K.O. filled in. "Raj's current sponsor won't be continuing. They overextended themselves trying to go public, so they have to pull back for a while. Alani knows Ryan Bauer and RC is always looking for fresh talent, so he's put them together."

"What are you, his agent now?" Maureen tended to get snarky when she felt left out of things.

"Pretty much." K.O. smiled. "I've been his agent while he's been here, and he's still alive. So you guys need to have a heart to heart with Raj. A lot of folks here think he's got what it takes to make the big time, so that takes planning."

K.O. decided *not* to tell Maureen everything that had happened. She decided a 'need to know' basis was more prudent. If the case came to trial, and if Raj was needed, then she'd inform her sister. However, a year is a long time and by that time all of this would be forgotten. Justine would be in college, Raj might be in Fiji surfing, who knew what would happen?

217

Chapter 14

The family spent the rest of Sunday on the beach; Raj supporting his fellow surfers along with the pink tee fan club. They ate huge plate lunches and all of Alani's snacks. It was chaotic and carefree and K.O. couldn't remember being this happy in a long time.

Raj garnered a lot of attention, not only from other kids, but from adults that K.O. thought were movers and shakers in the surf world. He was even interviewed up in the big stand. They couldn't go with him into the tiny space, but they'd get to see it later. Raj emerged glowing. Ryan Bauer made some initial overtures about signing Raj, and Maureen was steam-rolled into allowing him to try. K.O. enjoyed that part immensely. Joe and Alani were tasked with contracts and logistics, at least until they got professional consultation.

For a guy who lost a major contest, Raj was over the moon.

Justine enjoyed the male attention. Although she had just arrived from Seattle, her skin glowed with a slight tan, from her dad, not from the overcast skies of Washington. She'd gotten her mom's blonde hair, made muddy by daddy's genes, but green green eyes that impaled like lasers. *Yep, she'd gotten the family glare all right.* When she used it, which was often as a teenager, *it seared right into the back of your brain,* K.O. thought. But now, it served a different purpose, luring unsuspecting beach boys to their doom, buying her sodas and tee shirts. She basked in the attention. K.O. could tell Raj was relieved to have a distraction, not only for himself, but so he could talk pro surfing with the Rip Curl guy. Both mom and dad were in a tizzy deciding which chick needed protecting the most: the career kid or the Aphrodite of Ehukai Beach.

Finally, everyone wore down. Maureen begged that Raj go with them in their rental back to town. Justine was ripped from the arms of yet another muscled local boy, and Alani and K.O. packed up their beach kits. Maureen and Joe were staying at Kaneohe Bay Resort, not far from K.O.'s condo, so they agreed to meet for dinner later.

When they got back to K.O.'s condo, she and Alani were exhausted. Teresa was not amused at the lack of staff, so Alani took it upon himself to correct that. He got her fresh food and water and popped open a beer. When Teresa was satisfied, he picked her up and sat in the recliner and gave her a massage.

K.O. called dibs on the first shower, so when she finished, she got herself a beer and replaced Alani as cat massager while he took his shower.

"Better?" K.O. asked when he joined her, sitting on the arm of the recliner so he could scritch Teresa's chin properly.

"Way better. Was a great day," he added.

"Yes, it was. Thank you for being there and for putting up with my family." K.O. turned her face up for a kiss. He complied. He kissed her firmly, and then more softly. She put her beer down and wrapped her arms around him. It felt so good. Teresa jumped down in irritation. They were late meeting the family for dinner.

*　　　*　　　*　　　*

Dinner was loud and fun, and they fit right in at Ellie and Daniel's unfancy but amazing Chinese restaurant. Raj's choice. They rolled out all the special dishes, made just for his celebration. Justine pouted a little at being separated from all that well-formed testosterone so soon. They had to head back to Seattle tomorrow. Raj would stay on a few more days as planned, to watch the rest of the contest, make contacts, 'network' as he was learning to say. Then, in keeping with the original plan, K.O. would fly back with Raj for Christmas.

Chapter 15

K.O. and Raj saw the family off to the airport early since she had to get Raj up to the North Shore. She'd promised she'd be there for him, and although he wasn't competing any longer, she agreed it was beneficial for him to be a presence, show support for his BBB team and foster his new relationship with Rip Curl. Plus, it was fun.

They stood on the rise of golden sand, the center of a maelstrom of fans, photogs, noise and wild energy. K.O.'s heart was full. Full of pride, love, and all that goes with family. Her family wore her out, but certain members, Raj, Joe, and even Alani, who wasn't a legal member yet, *what? Where did that come from? They hadn't even discussed it, really.* They had danced around the topic, but neither had said actual words. Those guys gave her a sense of peace and belonging.

She refocused her thoughts and let the calming effects of Raj, Joe and Alani return. Better. Warmth filled her and she put her arm around Raj's waist and squeezed. To her surprise, he put his arm around her shoulders and squeezed back. They stood in a sideways hug for a moment.

"Auntie, you know you're da bes'."

"I know," K.O. answered.

"Ho! Dat!" Raj hollered, dropping his arm and pushing her away as he jumped straight up.

K.O.'s adrenaline raced down her spine. "What! Jeez, Raj."

"Auntie, didn't you see dat? Don't you pay attention to anyt'ing das important?"

She eyed him dancing in the sand, jubilant at someone's ride, and saw again, Raj at many ages and sizes. They would always be connected. She was sure of that.

"Yes, Raj. I do."

The End

Victoria Heckman's first *Hawai'i mystery series* features officer Katrina Ogden, K.O., of the Honolulu Police Department. Her second series, *Coconut Man mysteries of Ancient Hawai'i* begins with *Kapu-Sacred*. Her third mystery series (*Burn Out & Wet Work*) starring animal communicator Elizabeth Murphy is set on California's Central Coast. Stand alone mystery, *Pearl Harbor Blues,* begins on Dec. 7, 1941 and uncovers a dynasty of corporate intrigue. She belongs to Sisters in Crime-Central Coast Chapter. Visit her website www.victoriaheckman.com or find her on Facebook,Twitter & Instagram.

www.ingramcontent.com/pod-product-compliance
Lightning Source LLC
Chambersburg PA
CBHW031402250626
47155CB00004B/1381